Goddess Girls

ARTEMIS
THE BRAVE

**JOAN HOLUB &
SUZANNE WILLIAMS**

D1513783

www.atombooks.net/tween

ATOM

First published in the United States in 2010
First published in Great Britain in 2012 by Atom

Copyright © 2010 by Joan Holub & Suzanne Williams

The moral rights of the authors have been asserted.

A CIP catalogue record for this book
is available from the British Library.

ISBN 978-1-907411-49-6

Typeset in Baskerville by M Rules
Printed and bound in Great Britain by
Clays Ltd, St Ives plc

Papers used by Atom are from well-managed forests
and other responsible sources.

MIX
Paper from
responsible sources
FSC   FSC® C104740
www.fsc.org

Atom
An imprint of
Little, Brown Book Group
100 Victoria Embankment
London EC4Y 0DY

An Hachette UK Company
www.hachette.co.uk

www.atombooks.net/tween

For Cynthia Leitich Smith and Little Willow

J. H. and S. W.

CONTENTS

1

The Hunting Game

On silver-winged magic sandals, Artemis zoomed through the Forest of the Beasts, her feet gliding just a few centimetres above the mossy forest floor. "Come out, come out, wherever you are," she sing-songed under her breath.

Dodging tree trunks and ducking under low-hanging vines, she listened carefully for any unusual sounds. Her keen dark eyes searched the dense woods. Her favourite bow – its limbs made of curved, polished olive wood – was at the ready. A tooled leather quiver of arrows was slung across her back. She could pull one out and have it nocked and aimed in a split second, as soon as it was needed.

Behind her, Artemis heard Athena whizzing along in winged sandals as well. And following her were Aphrodite and Persephone. All four goddessgirls wore ankle-length flowing gowns called chitons, and their skirts whipped in the breeze as they zipped through the forest of olive, fig and pomegranate trees, their feet never quite touching the ground.

They had come here this afternoon for one purpose: to duel with some of the slimiest, smelliest beasts ever to roam the Earth. Armed with magic-tipped arrows, the goddessgirls had already defeated a she-dragon called Echidna and beaten a goat-headed Chimera. Now they had only ten minutes left to find the third beast they were tracking.

Winning this one final battle of good versus evil was critical. Something very important hung in the balance.

Their grades.

On the first Friday of every month, all the goddessgirls and godboys in their Beast-ology class left Mount Olympus Academy and came down to Earth. Here in this forest, for an entire hour, they played games of skill that Professor Ladon had created to test them. How lucky that Artemis and her best friends were in the same class and that they'd all been assigned to this section of the woods!

Defeating three beasts today would mean an A for each of the four girls. Getting only two was a B, one a C, and coming up empty meant having to repeat the test until they got it right. Artemis had never ever got less than an A in the Beast-ology games, and she didn't want this to be an exception. Today was her birthday, after all. Another A would be the perfect gift to herself.

As she entered a clearing, Artemis heard a snuffling sound. The grey-green leaves of a nearby grove of olive trees rustled, disturbing finches and warblers, which flew away in a great flutter of wings. She slowed, motioning silently to her friends to alert them that something was up.

"It's lurking. Over there!" Artemis called softly as the others drew up beside her. Just then the wind changed direction, and she got a whiff of the creature. *Ugh.* It smelled like pond weed, wet dog and cow pats all rolled into one.

4

Persephone groaned and fanned her hand in front of her naturally pale face, causing the fringe of her curly red hair to flutter. "Doesn't exactly smell like flowers, does it?" A skilled gardener, she could make anything bloom at the touch of a finger.

Athena wrinkled her nose. "No, it's more like a skunk."

"I hope it doesn't turn out to be something that slings slime this time," whispered Aphrodite. Flipping her long, shiny blonde hair over one shoulder, she touched the gold braid edging the neckline of her chiton. "This outfit is new and I don't want it ruined." The goddessgirl of beauty, she liked to dress well. She had an outfit for every occasion. This one was a bright robin's-egg blue that matched her eyes. Circling her slender waist was a belt made of woven grapevines. Since

5

Aphrodite set most fashion trends at Mount Olympus Academy, every goddessgirl at school would probably be wearing a belt just like it before the end of the week.

STOMP. STOMP. STOMP. The ground shook as the beast lumbered closer. Goosebumps rose on Artemis's arms. She'd rather eat a scarab beetle than admit it aloud, but she was scared. Because she was goddess of the hunt and was skilled at archery, everyone at school assumed she was brave. Her friends depended on her to lead them in these hunts. Even now the others were waiting for her to tell them what kind of beast they'd found. And she had a hunch she knew what it was!

Raising her left hand overhead, she held up one finger. Then, after a moment's pause, two fingers. Another pause. Three fingers. And finally, four.

Then, holding up her other hand, she showed two more fingers to make six in all. This signalled to the others that they'd probably found a one-headed, two-armed, three-bodied, four-winged, six-legged beast. Just in case they hadn't got the message, she silently mouthed the beast's name: *Geryon*.

At the news, Athena got the determined look on her face that she always had just before taking a test she wanted to ace. Persephone pinched her nose closed, as if preparing for the worst smell ever to get even worse as their opponent came closer. And Aphrodite glanced down at her stylish blue chiton, looking more than a trifle concerned.

Seconds later a giant creature jumped out of the woods into the clearing. At the sight of it, goosebumps rose on top of the goosebumps Artemis already had. The Geryon was big. It was bad. It was beastly. It looked just like the one whose features she'd memorised from her Beastology textscroll.

Although she loved to hunt, she wished they'd shoot at normal targets. Sometimes the beasts Professor Ladon designed for these tests seemed so ... so *real*. She struggled to remember that they were fake.

"You called this one right as usual," confirmed Athena from behind her. "Watch out, the class textscroll says they have particularly vicious talons and wily ways."

"And bad breath," added Aphrodite, holding her nose now along with Persephone.

The Geryon licked its green lips, eyeing them each in turn. Then it turned and waggled its three rear ends so its trio of long tails swept back and forth in the leaves. "Nah nah nuh *nah* nah," it taunted softly. All the while, its blazing red eyes watched them over its shoulder to see if they'd take the bait and move closer. When they didn't, it reached a hand towards them. It poked one foreclaw out and curled it over and over, beckoning them to follow it into the intricate maze of bushes beyond it known as the labyrinth. There was rumoured to be some sort of fantastical beast-making machine in the centre, which Professor Ladon had specially designed to spawn their opponents for these games.

"Ye gods," Athena whispered. "Does it really think we'll fall for that?"

"There's no way we're following it into that maze," Artemis agreed, her voice shaking. Then, worried that her words might have sounded cowardly, she added in a confident voice, "Let's try to lure it closer. I'd like to get a good shot at that big green bottom."

Persephone giggled, but with her nose pinched tight, it sounded more like a snore.

"Okay, but not too close," said Aphrodite, glancing nervously down at her chiton again. The beasts couldn't harm the goddessgirls, who were immortal, after all. Still, these horrible creatures had ways of making students ... uncomfortable. Artemis had had her hair singed once in Year Three, and had got a rash from a poisonous dart shot from a serpentine tail in Year Five.

"Let me try something," said Persephone. With that, she bent low to a bed of weeds, then blew across it. Seeds encased in fluffy puffs of white whooshed towards the beast. As if on cue, the creature began sneezing. And with each sneeze, it bounced a little closer to them.

Persephone grinned. "Dandelions. Geryons are allergic to them. Works every time."

Suddenly the beast stopped sneezing and let out a huge triple snort from its three giant, hairy nostrils. It planted both hands on its hips. Its eyes flashed red and beady on each of the goddessgirls in turn, as if it was trying to decide who to gobble up first.

"Uh-oh," said Athena. "Somebody looks annoyed."

"Quick! Fan out. As a group, we're too easy a target!" Artemis told them, trying to keep the panic she felt out of her voice. Not seeming to notice how breathless she sounded, the others took her direction and fanned out around the beast in a semicircle.

Persephone, who'd probably seen far more

fearsome creatures when she'd visited the Underworld with her friend Hades, kept her cool. "Got this one?" she called softly to Artemis.

Hovering just centimetres above the ground in her magic sandals, Artemis's fingers trembled as she slipped an arrow from her quiver. "Yeah, under control," she murmured with her usual show of bravado. She nocked the single arrow in her bow but didn't pull back the string quite yet. She didn't want to shoot one of her friends by accident! "C'mon, just a *little* closer," she crooned, eyeing the beast.

The Geryon's eyebrows bunched together like angry caterpillars. It gnashed its five green teeth and pawed its clawed hooves in the grass. But because they'd spread out, it couldn't seem to decide who to attack first.

That is, until Aphrodite piped up, "It's going to charge!" Even when she was terrified and shouting, her voice was as beautiful as she was. Drawn by its lovely sound, the Geryon's frightful gaze focused on her. Its lips curved in a gruesome grin. It gnashed and pawed a little more, but this time it was just for show. Clearly, it had chosen a victim. With a mighty lunge, it charged towards Aphrodite. She shrieked again, so scared that she dropped her bow. "It's c-coming!"

Artemis zipped towards her, moving sideways, always facing the Geryon head-on like Professor Ladon had taught them. *Never turn your back on a beast.* This was one of Mr Ladon's top ten rules. As the Geryon loomed closer, she pulled back her bowstring, aiming.

Oomph! Before she could shoot, she bumped into

something. A tree? No, it was Aphrodite! In a tangle of arms and legs, they tumbled to the ground. Although their sandals would whisk them away to safety once they stood, their flight-magic could only flicker listlessly as long as the girls lay sprawled on the moss.

Beside her, Aphrodite whimpered, totally vulnerable to attack without her bow. Artemis had managed to hold on to hers, but in the confusion, her arrow had popped from it to land a metre or so away. She heard Athena and Persephone calling to them to get up. But for the moment she was frozen, too scared to move. Her eyes locked with the Geryon's as it loomed closer. And closer. Its smell was even more horrific now, and she could feel the heat of its breath even from twenty metres away. She'd once read somewhere about a mortal who'd died of fright. Even though she knew that couldn't happen to her, at the moment it seemed very possible. Her heart pounded. A fine sheen of perspiration prickled the back of her neck. She had to do something!

From then on things began to happen quickly, yet they seemed to her to move in slow motion. The Geryon was only three metres away now. It leaped in the air, preparing to ruin Aphrodite's new chiton, lower the goddessgirls' grades, and generally wreak havoc.

Fighting down feelings of terror, Artemis sat up, nocked a new arrow, and squinched one eye shut to aim. She straightened her shaking fingers to release the bowstring.

Zzzzing!

Poof! The second her arrow reached it, the monster disappeared into thin air.

15

"Yes!" Artemis exclaimed, her confidence flooding back. "Right between its four eyes!"

Seconds later the Geryon sprang up again at the entrance to the labyrinth, an arrow sticking from its forehead. Grinning now, it calmly plucked out the arrow, tossed it away and bowed to them. "Congratulations, goddessgirls," it said in a tone that was almost friendly. "You have now achieved the eighth Level of the Arrow. Your excellent progress will be reported to Professor Ladon in your Beast-ology class at Mount Olympus Academy. Until next time . . ."

As its last word died away, the fearsome Geryon disappeared in a puff of purple smoke that hung over the labyrinth for a few moments like wispy fog.

"Another save by Artemis the brave!" Athena quipped, sounding relieved.

"Thank godness!" Aphrodite added gratefully as Persephone and Athena helped her to stand.

Artemis didn't comment. She was thinking about their praise, quite sure she didn't deserve it. Her? Brave?

"You okay?" Persephone asked.

"Oh, um, yeah, sure," said Artemis. As soon as she and Aphrodite regained their footing, their sandals' magic revived and they rose to hover a few centimetres from the ground like the other girls.

"Well, I'm not," said Aphrodite, examining her blue-lacquered fingernails with a tragic expression. "I broke a nail. I knew there was a reason Beast-ology was my least favourite class." Pulling a magic nail file from the cosmetic bag in her quiver, she held out her hand and let the file whisk expertly around her fingertips, making repairs.

"It's important, though," said Artemis. "Immortals have to learn this kind of stuff." It was true. Even if her courage did sometimes desert her without warning, she was glad the class was required. Putting two fingers between her lips, she whistled for her dogs. A bloodhound, a beagle and a greyhound came bounding towards her out of the forest.

"Good boy, Suez!" she told her bloodhound, who had retrieved one of her arrows. She'd named him after Principal Zeus – Suez was Zeus spelled backward – because like Zeus, Suez was big and blue-eyed. She hover-knelt a couple of centimetres from the ground to play with her dogs, and they bounded around her happily, their tongues hanging out.

Persephone crouched down lower too and joined Artemis. "Beast-ology is exciting. I'll say that for it," she said, as Amby, the beagle, gave her a slobbery

18

kiss. "Even though I know the mythical beasts aren't real, they look, smell and act so much like real monsters that it's hard to remember this is a lesson and they're only made of magic."

Athena held up both of her hands. "You've got that right. Look at my hands. They're still shaking. I was terrified, even though I knew that Geryon was a fake."

"But that's the whole point of Mr Ladon's game! He created the beasts to challenge our skill and bravery," said Artemis. She longed to admit that *her* hands had trembled too. It would have been a relief to share her fears, but the others had such confidence in her fearlessness that she was too embarrassed to do so. "It's great practice. You never know when a real beast will come along and need to be put in its place."

"Oh, come on. Have you ever seen even *one* real beast in your whole life?" asked Aphrodite. Studying her nails in satisfaction, she tucked the file away in her quiver. Then she pulled out a hand mirror and began primping, smoothing her hair and touching up her make-up.

"Well, no," Artemis admitted, standing again. In fact, she often wondered if she'd be up to the challenge of fighting a real beast, if she actually saw one. It was easy to appear brave and stay relatively cool when faced with *fake* beasts. But what if, when it really mattered, her bravery seriously failed her?

Just then a crooning sigh rippled over the forest, causing leaves to rustle and the moss that hung from the trees to sway. It was the gentle sound of the nymph girls who dwelled in the hawthorn, oak and willows. One by one, the nymphs began to peep out from behind the tree trunks and between branches, their pale faces glowing like fairy lights.

"The godboys must be coming," said Artemis, rolling her eyes. Nymphs were notoriously boy-crazy – the complete opposite of Artemis, who'd never had a crush on a boy in her entire life.

A soft smile curved Persephone's lips. "You're right. Here comes Hades."

Seconds later he appeared along with Artemis's twin brother, Apollo. Both had bows and quivers slung across their shoulders, since they were in the girls' Beast-ology class.

"How'd your hunt go?" called Apollo. Cruising closer on his winged sandals, he leaned in, banked, and did a dramatic swish that landed him next to Artemis.

"Nailed it," she assured him.

"Yes! Us too," said Apollo. They grinned and bumped knuckles.

The other goddessgirls might not be as into sports as Artemis was, but her twin loved archery just as much as she did. Unlike some siblings she'd read about, like Medea and Absyrtus or Romulus and Remus, the two of them had always got along. Probably because Apollo thought of her like a brother instead of a sister. Ever since she could remember, they'd played on all kinds of MOA sports teams together. They'd even trained for the Olympic games!

"Is Daphne here?" Apollo asked, eagerly looking around for the pretty nymph.

Artemis frowned at him. "Not you too." Lately it seemed like everyone at school was falling in love, or

22

at least in *like*. She lifted a brow in Aphrodite's direction. "This is all your fault." As the goddessgirl of love, as well as beauty, Aphrodite had a hand in just about every romance on Earth and on Mount Olympus.

Aphrodite flashed her a smile. "What can I say? It's spring! Love is in the air!" She leaned closer, her bright-blue eyes gazing straight into Artemis's blue-black ones. "One of these days, you'll meet a boy you like, and then you'll see for yourself how wonderful romance can be."

"Hah! I may be the goddess of the hunt, forest and moon, but I wouldn't be caught dead mooning over any godboy." Digging in her quiver, Artemis located a bag of dog treats and tossed them towards her hounds. All three scrambled to get them, managing to wolf the biscuits down in record time.

"You'll never be caught *dead* doing anything," Persephone reminded her, laughing. "We're goddessgirls. We're immortal!"

Hades smiled down at the petite, pale Persephone, looking amused by her little joke. Earlier in the school year, he'd been all frowns and troubles, but he seemed happier now that he and Persephone were such good friends. Maybe romance did work for some people, but Artemis just wasn't interested.

"See you back at school!" called Persephone. Holding hands, she and Hades took off together, winging their way up the mountain towards Mount Olympus Academy.

Just then Artemis heard a soft *ping! ping! ping!* sound. From far away, the voice of MOA's herald floated to their ears. "Lesson four at Mount Olympus Academy will commence in ten minutes."

"Oh, no! I can't be late for Hero-ology class!" said Athena. "And I need time to fix my hair."

"We all do," Aphrodite added. Putting her mirror away, she pointedly looked Artemis up and down.

"Let's take my chariot," said Artemis, oblivious to the hint. "It's faster than our sandals." None of the other students kept a chariot at school, but Zeus had made an exception for her after four deer had followed her back from a Year-Two field trip to Mount Parnassus in southern Greece. They'd become her pets and pulled her chariot ever since. Animals were always befriending her like that. Boars, goats, foxes – you name it. She'd even had a pet bear in Year Four, but eventually Principal Zeus had put his giant gold-sandalled foot down. She could only keep three dogs and four deer as pets, and that was that.

At Artemis's summons, four white deer with golden horns leaped from the forest, pulling her chariot behind them. "C'mon," she called to her companions. Jumping in, she took the reins. Everyone crowded in with her, including her hounds. The chariot lifted off, and together they whooshed from the forest and up the mountainside towards school.

2

The New Boy

The minute the chariot landed in front of Mount Olympus Academy, the deer magically unhitched themselves and leaped away to graze in the nearby gardens. Apollo and the three goddessgirls raced up the gleaming granite staircase that led to the majestic school. Built of polished white stone, MOA was five storeys tall and surrounded on all sides by many

Ionic columns. After they pushed through the bronze doors at the top of the stairs, they untied their winged sandals and tossed them into a communal basket. Slipping into their normal sandals, they went their separate ways, rushing to make it to class on time.

Artemis hurried down the hall to her locker, weaving among students who were chatting and visiting their lockers between classes. Her dogs romped at her heels, tongues hanging out, as they dashed and darted among sandalled feet. The hall was like an obstacle course to them, and dodge-the-students was one of their favourite games. Artemis tossed out a few "sorry"s and "excuse me"s on their behalf. But the dogs were completely oblivious to the startled and sometimes annoyed looks they were getting.

"Number one thirty-three, please open for me!" she called to her locker from a couple of metres away. She heard the click of its combination lock. Just as she skidded to a halt before the locker, its tall, skinny wooden door flew open.

Before she could catch them, the red textscroll from Hero-ology class and her sparkly pink *Goddessgirl Guide* both tumbled out. *Thunk! Thunk!* They hit the marble floor. She picked them up and tried to stuff them back into her already overflowing locker.

Thwack! A big bag of dog treats slipped from her locker, past her elbow, and just missed landing on her toes. The bag split on impact, sending colourful bone-shaped treats skittering in all directions. Suez and the other two dogs scampered after them, claws slipping and sliding on the slick floor. Soon they were chomping away, their bodies twisted together in a jumble of legs, noses and tails that resembled a pooch pretzel.

"Yikes!" someone exclaimed from behind her. Glancing over her shoulder, Artemis saw a blonde boy she didn't recognise skidding on the dry treats. Arms windmilling, he fought to regain his balance as her big hounds bumped him from all sides. Textscrolls and a bag flew from his hands, and he fell to his knees.

"Sorry!" she called to him. "Are you okay?"

"No!" Frowning darkly, he got to his feet. Treats crunched under his sandals as he started collecting his stuff from the floor.

"I *said* I was sorry," Artemis muttered. Since he looked unhurt, she turned her attention back to her locker. Holding a mound of stuff in place with one hand, she dug through the pile as best she could with her other.

"Beauty-ology textscroll? Are you in here?" she demanded. She cocked an ear to listen, but the scroll didn't reply. "Where could I have left that thing?" It better not be in her dorm room, she thought. There was no way she had time to dash up four floors to get it.

Behind her, the blonde boy headed for a locker just down from hers, but she didn't pay much attention. Stretching her neck to look past him, she managed to glimpse the sundial in the school courtyard through the window opposite the row of lockers. Only five minutes left till class started!

Didn't teachers understand that the trip from Earth to MOA took a while? Students should get extra time between classes on the days when they had Beast-ology hunts, but of course they didn't. Sometimes school rules stunk.

She sniffed the air. Something else kind of reeked too. She stuck her head inside her locker. Yuck. Was that the smell of an old lunch she'd stowed and forgotten? Well, she didn't have time to do anything about it now. Sooner or later it would stop smelling anyway – right?

Suddenly a dog she'd never seen before bounded up to her from out of nowhere. It was small, about the size of a cat, with long, glossy white fur. It raced around and around, barking.

Immediately forgetting her haste to get to class, she knelt and stroked its silky coat, which had a little blue bow tied in it. A feather pen and a few papers slid from her locker and fell unnoticed to the floor around her. "Oh! You're adorable. But who are you?" she asked, trying to get the dog to hold still long enough so she could read the star-shaped tag attached to the collar at his neck. Chiselled into the tag were the words: I BELONG TO ORION.

She flipped the tag over, but there was no more information. "Hmm. I don't see your name."

"Sirius," said a voice from close behind her. It was the boy who'd slipped on the dog treats.

"Yes, I'm serious. His name is totally missing from his tag."

"No, I mean that's his name. Sirius. He's mine." Reaching down, he gave the dog a fond pat and it began wiggling all over as if glad to see him.

"He's so cute." Straightening, Artemis stood to hand over the dog. She hadn't really looked at the boy properly before. But now, as she stood with his little dog in her arms, she looked up ... and up, into a pair of pale-blue eyes framed by the longest, darkest eyelashes she'd ever seen on a boy. He was taller than her by at least ten centimetres, and buff. "So I guess you must be . . . "

"Orion," he finished for her. Taking his dog, he set him on the floor, where he joined Artemis's hounds in wolfing down treats. Then, with a flick of his wrist, Orion undid the lock on the locker two down from hers. "I'm new here, as of today."

That explained why she'd never seen him before.

Orion swung his locker door open and stowed the five textscrolls he'd been holding. His skin shimmered slightly as he moved, as if he'd been powdered with a fine golden glitter. Only immortals, including Artemis and her goddessgirl friends, had skin that shimmered like that. So he was obviously a godboy.

Feeling strangely drawn to this good-looking boy, she took a half-step towards him. "I'm Artemis, goddess of the hunt." Why was he looking at her so oddly, as if something was wrong with her? Then he glanced sideways and eyed her open locker critically. She turned to stare at the jumble inside it too. "Um ... I was looking for my Beauty-ology textscroll. Goddess of the hunt, so I'm always hunting for stuff, you know?" Her little joke fell flat. Feeling embarrassed at the mess, Artemis tried to shut her locker door. It wouldn't close. Leaning her shoulder against it, she pushed with all her might, and finally the lock caught.

"If you cleaned it out once in a while, you might be able to find things," he said.

"I did clean it out," protested Artemis. Then she laughed. "Once. In Year Two."

Again, Orion didn't join in her laughter. She toyed with the GG charm necklace she and her friends all wore, as he neatly arranged the scrolls he'd stowed in his locker so they stood on end like small papyrus columns. As she watched, he pulled a mirror out of his bag and hung it on the inside of his locker door at eye level. Gazing at his reflection, he began styling his hair with his fingers, repairing the damage from his fall. His blonde hair stood up in spikes. How did he get it to do that? she wondered, fascinated.

Ruff! Ruff!

Her dogs had finished eating and were running up and down the halls, playing a game of chase with their new dog friend. "Quiet, guys! You'll get us all in trouble," she said, doing her best to shush them.

Orion was too busy studying his class schedule to

notice. Tucking it in his pocket, he pulled a lavender-coloured textscroll from his locker. Two small masks, one smiling and one frowning, dangled from the ends of the purple ribbon tied around it. They were the symbols of the theatre – comedy and tragedy.

As he shut his locker, Artemis nodded towards the scroll he'd chosen. "You're taking Drama class?"

"Uh-huh." His eyes brightened with sudden enthusiasm. "I've got quite a reputation as an actor and an orator back home. Maybe you've heard of me? Orion Starr? I'm here at MOA as a foreign exchange student. Invited by Principal Zeus himself."

"No, sorry. I don't really go to the theatre much except for sporting events," she admitted. Then, worried she might have hurt his feelings, she rushed on. "But I'm sure you must be an amazing actor if Zeus thinks so."

In response, Orion put a hand over his heart. A faraway expression came over his face.

"Are you okay?" Artemis asked, suddenly a little worried about his health.

Instead of answering, he swept his other arm out in a move as graceful as that of an Apollonian dancer. Gazing into the distance, he began to speak. "And now, Socrates, as you rebuked the vulgar manner in which I praised astronomy before, my praise shall be given in your own spirit. For every one, as I think, must see that astronomy compels the soul to look upwards and leads us from this world to another."

He stopped and grinned at her. "That's from *The Republic*, written by the philosopher Plato. Like it?"

Momentarily dazzled by his beaming white smile, Artemis mumbled, "Um, yeah." Though she wouldn't know a good actor from a bad one, what she'd just heard had sounded pretty impressive.

Ping! The final bell rang out. Lessons were going to start soon.

Orion half turned away, glancing down the now empty hall. "Guess I'd better get going," he said.

"Drama's that way. In the next wing," she told him, indicating which way he should go. Then, after a moment's hesitation, she added, "Want me to show you?" His class was in the opposite direction from hers, so she wasn't sure why she made the offer. But in spite of their rocky beginning – with him slipping on the dog treats and all – she had a feeling he might just turn out to be the most interesting boy she'd ever met, aside from Apollo.

She wanted to keep talking to him, and she didn't care if that made her late for her own class.

"Sure, thanks." Orion whistled and his dog came bounding over. He scooped him up and the dog began licking his chin. He grinned, patting Sirius's furry white head, and set him back down. "He adores me – what can I say?"

It was kind of cool that he liked dogs as much as she did. She wondered what else they might have in common. As they walked down the hall together, their four dogs trotted along beside them.

"I forgot to introduce my hounds," said Artemis. "This is Suez. That's Zeus spelled backwards. And the beagle is Amby, named after ambrosia, my favourite food. And this is my greyhound, Nectar, named after – well, nectar." She pointed to each dog in turn as she spoke.

"Interesting," he said, but he didn't sound like he was really listening.

"What kind of dog is Sirius?"

"A Maltese." He started walking a little faster.

"Oh." She sped up too and began to speak more rapidly, trying to hold his attention. "I've never seen a belt like that before," she said, pointing to the three stars on his buckle.

"These are actually acting awards." Slowing a bit, Orion touched each star in turn. "This is the Alnitak, next is the Alnilam, and finally the prestigious Mintaka award."

Though she'd never heard of those awards, Artemis nodded politely. "Nice." When he didn't say anything else, she filled the silence, babbling all the way to his classroom. She didn't know why she had such a strong urge to make herself interesting to this boy, especially since he didn't seem all that interested in *her*.

"Well ... " he said as they reached the drama room. Again he studied her face and hair, as if he thought her odd. What was he looking at exactly? Did he think she was cute? And why did she care? She'd never felt like this before around a boy – sort of jittery and excited and not sure why. Had he put some kind of "liking" spell on her? If he had, it was working.

Beside the door, Artemis noticed a poster about the upcoming school play, called *The Arrow*. She gestured towards it. "Are you going to try out?"

"Of course," he said. "I was the lead in every play in Larissa Middle School back home. I've been acting since nursery, when I was the lead mushroom in *Boy Heracles.*"

Sirius began barking as Orion started to open the door. He sighed and picked up his dog, then turned back to her. "Hey, would you mind keeping those midnight-blues pinned on my dog for a while?"

"Huh? Midnight-blues?"

"Your eyes – they're the colour of midnight. Not quite black, not quite blue."

"Oh." Artemis felt her cheeks burning sunset pink. No one had ever said that about her eyes before.

"So I was asking if you'd watch Sirius? It's my first day, and I've got a lot to do. I don't really have time for him." Orion smiled at her with his twinkling eyes. How could she say no?

She sighed, feeling a silly smile curving her lips. "No problem," she heard herself say.

"Thanks." He winked and handed Sirius to her. "Catch you later."

Artemis and the four dogs just stood there, watching him disappear inside the classroom. The little Maltese whined when he could no longer see his master. "I know how you feel, boy," she told him. Orion was like bright fireworks, mesmerising and spectacular. The hallway seemed somehow dimmer with him gone. "Looks like you'll be hanging out with me and my hounds today. Let's go." She gave him a pat and set him on the floor.

Then she remembered she'd never found her Beauty-ology textscroll. Maybe her teacher wouldn't notice if she went to class without it. And by some miracle, maybe she wouldn't notice that Artemis was late either.

3

The Crush

"You're late, Artemis, dear. And where's your textscroll?" a voice asked the minute she entered Beauty-ology class. Her teacher, Ms Three-Graces, spoke in elegant, soothing tones, even when she was annoyed. And she was impeccably groomed as always, her hair, chiton and make-up as perfect as if she had dressed for a fashionable dinner party instead of to teach a class.

"Um, I couldn't find it in my locker. It's kind of messy in there, I guess," Artemis replied as she shut the door.

When she turned around again, the teacher eyed her more closely and gasped. "My godness! What happened to you? Have you been in an accident?"

"Huh? No, why?" asked Artemis.

After obviously searching for a tactful way to express herself, Ms Three-Graces finally said, "You don't look yourself."

Artemis hurried over to a bronze make-up mirror in the cosmetology area and glanced at her reflection. *Gods-a-mighty!* She was a mess! Her hair was tangled with twigs. There was dirt on her cheek. Well, Aphrodite had tried to tell her to fix her hair, but since she was always trying to give everyone makeovers, Artemis hadn't understood that this time she really needed one. No wonder Orion had looked at her so oddly. How embarrassing!

Turning away from the mirror, she rubbed at the dirt on her face and finger-combed the twigs from her hair. Then she paused. Since when did she care what a boy – mortal or immortal – thought of her? Then again, Orion *was* kind of cute. Handsome, really. The handsomest boy she'd ever seen, in fact. He didn't seem as goofy as most other boys. And he liked dogs. A big plus.

She was shocked to hear herself actually sigh. She sounded just like the nymphs when Apollo and Hades had entered the forest earlier that day. Boy crazy.

Artemis left the cosmetics area and went to sit at

her desk, but her unsettling thoughts went with her. She'd never had a crush on *any* guy before. Everybody knew that. So what if Orion liked dogs? So what if he was as gorgeous as the mortal Narcissus? She knew plenty of other boys who liked dogs, and most godboys were handsome. Why him?

As she took her seat, Orion's image leaped to mind again: the pale-blue eyes, the long dark eyelashes, the tall, muscular build, the spiky blonde hair. Together with his obvious dramatic skill, those traits certainly seemed to suggest a kind of star quality. She smiled dreamily. Why *not* him? Maybe like Aphrodite said, she was about to find out how wonderful romance could be.

"Artemis!" The teacher's voice jerked her back to attention. "Where's your mind today?" Uh-oh. Ms ThreeGraces was standing right beside her desk.

Artemis looked round. Everyone else was busy working. How long had she been daydreaming? Glancing down at her desk, she saw she'd been drawing hearts on her papyrus notescroll instead of taking notes.

"Sorry, Ms Three-Graces."

"Really, Artemis." Glancing at the hearts on Artemis's notescroll, her teacher raised a perfectly shaped eyebrow. "Since you've forgotten your textscroll and can't follow today's assignment, you may write a three-page essay on the beauty of being organised instead."

Ugh, thought Artemis. "You mean now?" Ms ThreeGraces looked at her sternly. With a sigh, Artemis picked up her quill pen and began to write. Although Ms Three-Graces was okay, Artemis liked Beauty-ology class about as much as Aphrodite liked

Beast-ology hunts. And although the lesson seemed to drag on longer than usual today, she wasn't able to get her assignment done before the bell rang. After rolling up the half-finished papyrus, she dashed out of the room with it before her teacher could ask her to stay till it was finished.

As she always did on Friday afternoons once school was out, Artemis met her brother Apollo in the Coliseum arena for archery practice. But today she brought Sirius along with her own hounds. As soon as she arrived, the dogs began to frolic together in the park nearby, traipsing through fields of asphodel, irises and ferns.

"Who's that?" asked Apollo when she showed up with the little white dog in tow. "I thought Principal Zeus said you could only keep three dogs in your room."

"His name is Sirius, but he's not mine. I'm dogsitting," said Artemis, pulling an arrow from her quiver. "Come on, let's shoot to see who's best out of ten."

"You're on." Apollo nocked his first arrow, forgetting all about the dog.

After two hours of target practice, they packed up their archery equipment and headed to the cafeteria for dinner. The dogs trailed after them, ready for dinner as well. When they got to the door, they found a ten-centimetre-long magic arrow darting around just outside.

"Artemis and Apollo?" it asked in a buzzy voice that was sort of like what a bumblebee might've sounded like if it could speak. Suez stood on his hind legs and put his front paws on the door, sniffing at the arrow interestedly.

Artemis looked at Apollo, who shrugged, looking blank. "Yes," she replied to the arrow. "That's us."

The arrow started buzz-talking again. "*Artemis and Apollo . . . I ask you to follow . . . me up the stairway . . . for a very . . .*"

"For a very what?" asked Artemis, bewildered when it didn't say more.

"*Follow me . . . and you'll see,*" buzzed the arrow, sounding a trifle impatient.

Apollo opened the door. "Come on. Let's find out what's going on."

"Okay, but I'm starving, so there had better be food involved in whatever's up there," Artemis warned the arrow. At that, the arrow zipped inside, leading them up the winding staircase. Taking the four dogs with them, they followed until they reached another door. Apollo pushed it wide, and they stepped into the open-air domed cupola at the top of the school.

"Happy birthday!"

"Wh-what?" Artemis jumped at the sound of lots of voices. The cupola was crowded with their classmates, including Aphrodite, Athena and Persephone, and some of Apollo's friends. There were balloons everywhere, and a small pile of gifts. Doves wove among the columns that encircled the dome, pulling colourful streamers behind them. The arrow that had led them there zipped into the room and took a nosedive into something that was set on a nearby table, joining more arrows just like it.

"You didn't think we'd forgotten, did you?" asked Aphrodite.

"No," said Artemis, "but *I* almost did. And I

certainly didn't expect all this. Thanks, you guys."
She gave her three best friends a hug. They all
hugged Apollo too. Then his godboy friends came
over to tease him about it. Eyeing the snacks,
Artemis scooted towards the table. Her dogs were
already there, sniffing around for any tasty crumbs
that might have fallen on the floor.

Set on a long marble table were terracotta bowls
of ambrosia, cups of nectar punch and hero
sandwiches. But what caught her eye was the large
round cake. It was decorated like a target, with
concentric circles of white, black, blue, red and
yellow icing. Stuck tip-first in the yellow bullseye at
its centre were thirteen arrows. As she and Apollo
approached, the end of each arrow suddenly blazed
with light. They were candles, she realised. She was
the first of her friends to turn thirteen.

"We made your cake in Ms ThreeGraces' class this morning," said Aphrodite.

"It looks really great," said Apollo, obviously impressed.

After they'd blown out the candles, Artemis hovered over the cake, trying not to drool. "So when do we cut it?"

Persephone laughed. Everyone knew Artemis had a sweet tooth. "How about now?"

At her words, each of the arrows slid out of the middle of the cake, neatly cutting it into slices. "Let's eat!" said Artemis, first in line to pile up her plate. Every time a slice was taken, another magically appeared in its place to complete the cake again.

Her hounds had a sweet tooth too, and so, apparently, did Orion's dog. When a couple of party-goers left their cake unattended, the dogs quickly helped themselves, smearing icing on their muzzles and leaving crumbs all over the floor, which they quickly slurped up. "Oops, I forgot you guys," Artemis said, scurrying over to find healthier snacks for them.

After everyone had eaten, Athena brought out two identical boxes. Both were long and slender. She handed the one tied with a gold ribbon to Apollo, and the box with the silver ribbon to Artemis. "We thought that with the archery competition coming up, you two would find these useful," said Aphrodite.

Artemis opened her box excitedly. Inside, she found three shiny arrows. "Silver arrows!" she breathed reverently. Glancing over at her brother, she saw that he'd got three golden ones.

"They're aerodynamically perfect," said Athena. "I designed the specifications for them, and Hephaestus helped Aphrodite make them in MOA's blacksmith workshop."

Hearing his name, Aphrodite's friend came over. "The first one is named Opsis," Hephaestus said, leaning on his cane. "That means 'aim'; the second is Loxos, or 'trajectory'; and the third is Hekaergos, which means 'distancing'."

"They'll smell good too," said Persephone. "I added perfume, so each one has a natural floral scent when it flies."

"Wow," said Artemis, stroking them lovingly.

Apollo glanced at Persephone in alarm. "No perfume on mine, I hope."

She laughed. "No, yours are designed to play the songs your band performs. Dionysus helped with that." Apollo's band was called Heavens Above, and it played at all the school dances.

Artemis was so overwhelmed she almost started to cry. Instead she held one arrow up and sighted down it. "It's straight and true. And the best gift I've ever had. Oh! Thank you so much." Jumping up, she gave her friends another round of hugs. As if worried they might be missing out on something, the four dogs leaped around the girls and tried to squeeze between them. Artemis laughed and hugged them too.

"So – what are you going to do this weekend?" Athena asked Artemis and Apollo when things settled down. "Something fun for your birthday? Maybe go to Poseidon's water park down on Earth?"

"Or maybe to the Olympic footraces," Apollo mused. "What do you think, Artemis?"

"Well … actually, I was thinking I might go and watch the auditions for the school play," Artemis announced. "They're tomorrow."

Apollo laughed as he went for seconds on the cake. "Ha! Good one. That'll be the day."

"I'm serious," said Artemis. "I want to see the auditions."

Apollo's jaw dropped, a fork halfway to his mouth. "Why the sudden interest in Drama?"

"Why not?" Artemis leaned over to pick up Sirius. He'd been pawing at her leg, and she wondered if he was feeling homesick for Orion and a bit overwhelmed by all this excitement.

"Don't tell me you got another dog?" Aphrodite said in horror. Apparently, she hadn't noticed Sirius until just that moment. That made sense. She'd never been overly fond of dogs and tried to ignore them. "He's not mine," Artemis assured her. "I'm only watching him for a friend."

"On your birthday?" asked Athena, sounding surprised.

"For who?" Persephone said at the same time.

"For the new godboy, Orion," said Artemis. "Have you met him yet? He's a foreign exchange student."

Apollo, who had begun playing a game of darts with Hephaestus, Hades and Dionysus, looked over. With a frown, he said, "Orion's not a godboy. Did he tell you he was?"

"Well, no," said Artemis, shaking her head. But he had to be. He was totally handsome and had glittery skin!

"He's a mortal," said Apollo.

Artemis's eyes widened. "Really? But he's so ... shimmery."

Apollo folded his arms, looking superior. Behind him, the darts game continued. "Have you been to the Immortal Marketplace lately? There's a new store there called Play Spray."

"I've heard of it!" Aphrodite said. "They sell all kinds of temporary body sprays and paints."

Apollo nodded. "Right. Orion told us he bought a bottle of something called GodBod and sprayed himself with it." He snapped his fingers. "Instant shimmer skin."

"Fake shimmer to look like us?" Persephone said, shaking her head. "What will those mortals think of next?"

"Imitation is the sincerest form of flattery," quoted Athena.

Sirius had begun to squirm in Artemis's arms, so she set him down. He scampered over to join her hounds in licking up the last bits of icing from abandoned plates. "How do you know all this?" she asked her brother.

"Orion told me himself. He's in my Olympics-ology class," said Apollo.

"I remember passing him in the hall this morning," Persephone added. "He didn't speak when I said hello. I thought he must be a little shy."

"Shy? Are you kidding? He's a bigmouth," said Apollo. "When Coach Triathlon asked him to tell us a little about himself, he went on and on for at least ten minutes."

"What did he say?" Artemis couldn't help asking.

Apollo rolled his eyes. "I don't know. I zoned out after the first minute. Something about his dreams of being a star."

"A star?" Persephone asked, looking towards the heavens in confusion.

"The actor kind," Apollo clarified. Turning towards the dartboard, he rejoined the game.

"He's probably trying out for the play tomorrow in the amphitheatre then," said Aphrodite. She eyed Artemis speculatively. Had she guessed the real reason for her sudden fascination with the theatre?

"I saw a poster about it. It's called *The Arrow*," said Artemis quickly. "Naturally, anything about archery catches my eye."

"I heard about it too." Persephone glanced at Athena, whose dad was the principal. "Principal Zeus is directing it, isn't he?"

Athena nodded. "It's a drama about Eros and Psyche."

"I'm hoping to snag the lead role," said a godboy

with eyes the colour of purple grapes. A talented actor, Dionysus took the lead in every school play. He was famous down on Earth too. There was even a dramatic festival held every year in Athens, Greece, in his honour.

Aphrodite smiled at him. "I wonder if you'll get the part?"

Dionysus grinned and shrugged, running his fingers through his curly black hair and around the two small horns that stuck up from the top of his head.

"Maybe I'll try out too," said Aphrodite. "I'd love to play Psyche, the nymph."

"We could help with the sets," Persephone suggested to Hades.

"Sure," he agreed distractedly, intent on aiming his dart.

"I'm already involved," said Athena. "Dad asked me to lead the Greek Chorus with my flute."

"Yes!" Apollo cheered Hades' dartboard bull's-eye, then turned to Athena. "Is this play a tragedy or a comedy?"

"A little of both, I think." She glanced from him to Artemis. "Maybe the two of you should try out. Dad mentioned he'll need some actors skilled in archery."

"Now that would *really* be tragedy," said Apollo. "Neither of us could act our way out of a papyrus bag."

"Speak for yourself," said Artemis. Secretly, she thought he was probably right though.

Her brother laughed. "Do whatever you want, but I'll stick to archery on the field, thanks. There are plenty of other good archers who'll try out, like Dionysus."

After that, talk drifted to other things, and eventually the party broke up. That night in her dorm room, Artemis spent some time finishing the essay on organisation that Ms Three-Graces had given her. Glancing around her messy room, she doubted the assignment would actually change anything. She was just naturally disorganised. Most of the time she couldn't be bothered to hang up her clothes. And what was the point of making her bed or cleaning out her locker anyway? They'd just get messy again. If she could've changed the title of her paper to "The Beauty of Being *Dis*organised," it would have been much easier to write!

By bedtime, Orion still hadn't come for his dog, and Sirius was acting kind of worried. Every time he heard footsteps in the hall outside Artemis's room, his head snapped up eagerly, and he cocked his ears towards the door. After the steps passed, his furry chin sank onto his front paws again, and he practically sighed with longing. Artemis was going to scold Orion tomorrow for deserting his poor pooch on his first day in a new place.

But maybe she'd wear her most fashionable chiton – if she could find it – and comb her hair to do it. Just so he'd see she wasn't always a mess.

4

Auditions

The next morning Artemis put on her best red chiton, which she found in a heap on the floor. As she hunted around for her belt, she stepped on something. "Ow!" It was a hair clip Aphrodite had given her years ago, hidden under an old, holey chiton she wore as a nightie. The clip was pretty. Why hadn't she ever worn it before? Gathering her hair high on her head, she clasped the gold band around it, then put on her belt and grabbed her bow and arrows. She didn't have a mirror, so she looked at her reflection in the sunlit window glass. She looked ... nice. But she couldn't help noticing that even her best chiton was a little wrinkled. And what was that spot on the shoulder? She angled the strap of her quiver to cover it and smoothed out the wrinkles as best she could.

Satisfied, Artemis whistled for Sirius and her hounds. "Let's go, guys!" Together, they hurried towards the amphitheatre where the drama auditions were being held. The dogs were in their usual high spirits, running this way and that and chasing everything that moved. Sirius seemed to have formed an attachment to Amby, the beagle, and playfully nipped at his tail and ears. When

Amby had had enough and started to chase him, Sirius dodged under the larger dogs, as if he were passing under tall bridges. "Hey, you guys, behave yourselves!" she exclaimed when they almost knocked her over. By the time they arrived, most of the seats were full and auditions were underway.

As she started down the aisle, Principal Zeus's voice thundered out. "Well?" Startled, she jumped. But then she realised he was only speaking to the actors.

More than two metres tall, with bulging muscles, a curly red beard and piercing blue eyes, Zeus was an intimidating sight. Wide, flat, golden bracelets encircled his wrists, and he always wore a belt decorated with a thunderbolt. Like most of the students at MOA, Artemis was just a little bit afraid of him.

The school herald consulted the scroll he held.

Then he struck the lyrebell with the tiny hammer he always carried. *Ping! Ping!* "Pandora and Dionysus, please report to the stage for auditions!" he called in his clear voice.

Spotting Aphrodite on a stone bench in the third row, Artemis went to sit with her. To her surprise, Apollo was seated one row behind with Hephaestus, Poseidon and some other godboys. Since when were they interested in Drama?

Taking a seat, she told the dogs to lie down. Tired from all their play, they didn't object. Suez curled up with his head on her feet, and the other three spilled over into the aisle to her left. Aphrodite shifted to her right, as far from the dogs as she could manage. Meanwhile, Pandora and Dionysus came onstage as directed.

Artemis leaned back to whisper to Apollo,

"What's up? I thought you weren't going to try out for the archery scenes."

"I thought the same thing about you."

"Me? I'm just here to watch. And to support Aphrodite when it's her turn. And to give Orion his dog."

"Yeah? Well, I'm just here to support Dionysus when he tries out, so—"

"Places!" Principal Zeus boomed, drawing everyone's attention. Apollo and Artemis both jumped in their seats, and onstage Pandora jerked in surprise, dropping her script.

"Stage left!" Zeus ordered as Pandora retrieved it. Frowning slightly, the herald leaned over and whispered to him. "Oh, yeah, I get those confused," Zeus replied. "I meant stage right!" he called to the actors.

"So how's it going?" Artemis asked Aphrodite.

"Three have tried out. I'll go last, after Pandora. She wants to play Psyche too. There are five of us trying out for the lead."

"What about the part of Eros?" asked Artemis, hoping she hadn't missed Orion's turn to try out for the boy lead.

"Five are trying out for that too." Suddenly Aphrodite's eyes swept over Artemis, taking in her styled hair and fancy chiton. "Hey! You look nice."

"Thanks." Artemis wanted to ask about Orion, but she didn't want to arouse Aphrodite's suspicion. Aphrodite was an expert at sniffing out any hint of romance, and it would be just like her to make Artemis's interest in Orion into some big deal. Which it wasn't. Not really.

Somewhere in the distance, she heard the sound

of chanting voices and music. Hidden from sight behind the stage backdrop, students had begun practising for the Greek Chorus that was part of every theatrical play. Their job was to narrate the story as it took place, to help the audience to understand what was going on. And, according to her Music-ology teacher back in Year Four, to explain the themes and deeper meanings of certain events. As the chorus chanted their lines to gentle music, the beautiful notes from Athena's flute were unmistakable.

At the back of the stage, students wielded paint-brushes or hammers, creating backdrops and scenery. Persephone was painting asphodel, daisies and daffodils on a green hillside, and Hades was painting great curls of fire spewing from a dragon's mouth.

"All right, cue the nymph!" Zeus boomed.

Situated at the right side of the stage now, Pandora jumped again at the crack of his deep voice. "Who? Me?" She nervously patted her fringe, which was shaped into a question mark.

"Yes, you. When I say 'cue,' it means you are to begin," Zeus explained, tapping his sandalled foot with impatience.

Nodding nervously, Pandora turned to Dionysus. Holding her script in one hand, she laid her other hand over her heart. "Oh, Eros, god of love, do not wound me with your arrows?"

"The wound will only make you fall in love, nothing more," Dionysus assured her. Though he'd spoken quietly, his voice seemed to fill the room with its power and beauty. Even Artemis, who had never been to a play in her life, could tell he was a good actor.

"I trust you not?" Pandora said, fluttering her eyelashes at him. "For I am but a nymph and therefore not immortal?"

"Very nice, you two," Zeus interrupted. "But, Pandora, please try not to turn every line you read into a question."

Pandora glanced at him in surprise. "Oh, sorry, Principal Zeus, was I doing that? I wonder why I didn't notice?"

Zeus's broad shoulders went up and down slightly and Artemis had a feeling he was sighing. She knew how he felt. Pandora was sweet, but her non-stop questions and curiosity got on Artemis's nerves sometimes too. Poor Athena actually had to live with Pandora though, because the two of them were roommates.

Before long, Pandora and Dionysus's audition

was over. As they left the stage, Zeus nodded in the herald's direction. In response, the herald struck his lyre bell again. *Ping!* "Aphrodite and Orion, please report to the stage for your audition!" he called out.

"Wish me luck," said Aphrodite, smoothing her seafoam-coloured chiton as she stood.

"Knock 'em dead," said Artemis. A dozen other godboys and goddessgirls called to wish Aphrodite luck too as she made her way to the stairs at the left side of the stage. She was the most popular girl in school. Especially with the godboys, who practically fell over themselves to catch her attention. In Artemis's opinion, she was a cinch for the part.

But that would mean that if Orion got the part of Eros, he and Aphrodite would spend a lot of time together. Hmm. Artemis couldn't help noticing that Aphrodite's chiton wasn't wrinkled and didn't have stains. She looked glamorous, something Artemis could never hope to be. What if Orion decided he liked Aphrodite? Artemis didn't like that idea one bit.

Orion entered the stage from the stairs at the opposite side. At the sight of him, Artemis sat up straighter. Her pulse raced a little faster. Her stomach did an unfamiliar little flip.

"Artemis," said Apollo, nudging her shoulder from behind. "How about if we go and get in some archery practice before—"

"Shhh!" she said, batting him away. Her eyes were glued to Orion as he sauntered onto the stage. His golden skin shimmered, his blue eyes twinkled, his broad shoulders looked even broader than she remembered in the turquoise toga he wore. Suddenly she wished she'd sat closer to the action.

"Artemis?" It was Apollo again. Why was he being so annoying all of a sudden?

"Later," she said, fluttering her hand to brush him off. "I want to stay to hear Ori–, um, I mean, Aphrodite audition. And I thought you wanted to support Dionysus," she reminded him. "He doesn't have the part yet, you know."

Apollo sighed and sat back, obviously bored. "Okay, but I doubt they need us. They always get the leads."

"You'll both begin reading on page ten," Zeus said, holding out scripts to the two new actors. Aphrodite took hers and thumbed through it to the correct page, but Orion held up the flat of his hand, refusing to take his.

Zeus frowned. "Go on, take it. You'll need the script to read your lines."

"Not necessary, Principal Zeus," Orion assured him. "I've already memorised the part of Eros." At the sound of Orion's voice, Sirius sat up, ears pricked. His tail began thumping. But he must have been accustomed to sitting in a theatre audience, because he didn't lunge for the stage to greet his master.

"Well, that's very professional of you," said Zeus, looking surprised. "You can begin then."

Pandora slid onto the bench beside Artemis, just as Orion opened his mouth to speak. Before he could utter a word, a banging sound came from the back of the stage. Hades had begun hammering green scales onto the dragon's tail.

Orion turned to glare at him. "Do you mind?"

"Sorry, artist at work," replied Hades, grinning to display the nails gripped between his teeth.

"Artists are at work here too," said Orion. "Thespians. Show some respect."

Hades looked a little embarrassed, but he stopped hammering. "Okay. No problem."

"Wow, who's that?" Pandora whispered to Artemis, nodding towards Orion.

"The new foreign exchange mortal from Earth," said Artemis.

"He's mortal?" A mortal herself, Pandora looked at him with even more interest. "Then why does he shimmer?"

"Fake shimmer spray," Apollo muttered from behind them.

Artemis ignored him. All around her, she heard other goddessgirls oohing and aahing over the new boy. Unfortunately, she wasn't the only one who found him intriguing.

Suddenly Aphrodite's voice filled the room. "Oh, Eros, god of love, do not wound me with your arrows." Her voice was as beautiful as she was, and Artemis could almost feel everyone's interest perk up when they heard her.

Orion took a deep breath, his muscular chest expanding. Then, in a smooth, emotion-filled voice, he replied, "The wound will only make you fall in love, nothing more." He reached out a hand and touched her cheek, as if he was trying to comfort her.

For a second Aphrodite just stood there, looking at him in surprise. He'd amazed even her with his talent. He was that good. No wonder Zeus had invited him to MOA to join the theatre!

"Aphrodite?" Zeus prompted.

She started, turning pink. "Oh, sorry, Principal Zeus."

"I trust you not," she went on, slipping back into the part of Psyche again. "For I am but a nymph and therefore not immortal."

"Wow! Aren't they great?" Pandora whispered.

Nodding, Artemis leaned forward to hear better. Planting her elbows on her knees, she rested her chin on her fists and listened to Aphrodite and Orion continue their lines. Their voices were almost like music, hers high, his low, both intertwining. For the first time, she understood, at least a little, why people liked plays.

After the two of them stopped speaking their lines a few minutes later, there was a small silence. Then the audience erupted in applause. Artemis blinked, straightening in her seat and glancing around. She'd been so caught up in their acting that she'd almost forgotten it was an audition, not the actual play.

Zeus had allowed them to read far more than the other actors who'd tried out.

"That was a mighty powerful performance," he said, sounding impressed. He looked at Orion. "Haven't seen you here before. Are you a new student?"

Orion appeared a little confused. "Um, yes, you invited me to come here, remember?"

"Huh?" Now it was Zeus's turn to look confused. "I remember inviting a mortal boy named Orio Snar—"

"I prefer to go by Orion Starr," Orion interrupted hurriedly. Seeming flustered, he added, "That's my stage name. Didn't you get the copy of my CV from the Thespian Guild of Earth? I gave it to the nine-headed lady in your office yesterday."

Zeus shrugged. "Maybe. My desk's piled with

stuff. I'm pretty busy, what with being King of the Gods, Ruler of the Heavens, and principal of MOA and all."

Artemis smiled. She liked knowing that Zeus was messy, just like her. It gave her hope. After all, messiness hadn't held Zeus back from becoming the most important god on Mount Olympus!

"I just happen to have another copy." Orion jumped down from the stage and grabbed a scroll from one of the chairs. Going over to Zeus, he unrolled the papyrus, pointing to various items. "As you see, I was the lead in Sophocles' tragedy *Electra* and in Euripides' *Medea* ... " As he went on, the other students began to shift and grow restless.

"What a show-off," muttered Apollo.

"He's just trying to let Zeus know he has experience," Artemis said, frowning at him over her shoulder. Couldn't Apollo give him the benefit of the doubt? Orion really wanted this part and probably had no idea he was coming across badly, reciting his long list of credits. Later, maybe she could find a tactful way to tell him that he didn't need to convince anyone how great he was. It was obvious!

"Can you shoot?" Principal Zeus butted in.

"Shoot?" Orion echoed.

"In the play, Eros shoots magic arrows," Zeus reminded him. "How are you at archery?"

"Oh, um, well, naturally I'm an expert marksman. Unfortunately, I don't have my bow with me," said Orion.

Apollo stood up. "You can borrow mine," he offered, picking it up from the bench beside him and holding it out.

From somewhere in a far row, Artemis heard Ares, a godboy who could sometimes be a bully, snigger. "Great idea!" he called out. "You should take him up on it, Orion."

Artemis twisted to glare at him and her brother. Apollo never let anyone touch his bow. He was obviously trying to embarrass Orion, hoping he was a poor shot. And Ares was egging him on. Sometimes godboys could be so annoying.

Orion froze like a deer in torch-lights, but then he quickly replied, "I'm not comfortable using someone else's bow. But thanks for the offer."

"I didn't mean now, anyway," Zeus explained. "Come by my office sometime this week, and you can give me a demonstration."

"Sure. No problem," Orion said, confident once more.

Zeus gestured to the MOA herald, who announced, "Auditions for supporting roles will now begin!" *Ping!*

As another group of actors came onstage to read for supporting roles, Orion headed off. Artemis jumped up. "I have to give Orion his dog," she told Apollo. "Back in a minute, and then we can go and practise." Before he could object, she smoothed her short, dark hair and straightened her chiton, then slung her quiver and bow over one shoulder. "Come on, boys," she said, shooing the dogs from their seats. Urging them down the aisle ahead of her, she kept an eye on Orion as she headed in his direction.

Sirius scampered ahead. When Artemis was still a few metres away, Orion's dog leaped into his arms and began happily nuzzling his face.

"I came to return your dog," Artemis said, once Sirius had calmed down.

"Huh?" Orion blinked, looking at her like he'd never seen her before.

"I'm Artemis, goddess of the hunt? Two lockers over from yours? You asked me to watch Sirius yesterday? I showed you to Drama class?" Godness, with all those question marks in her voice she sounded like Pandora!

Suddenly he seemed to notice the bow and quiver of arrows slung over her shoulder. His blue eyes gleamed with interest. "Oh, yeah. I remember now. Hey, are you any good with that?"

"My bow?" she asked, seeing the direction of his gaze. "Yep, I'm the best. Except maybe for my brother Apollo." She glanced towards the bleachers and saw that her brother was talking to some of his friends.

"Want to practise together sometime?"

Artemis's head whipped around to Orion again. He favoured her with a dazzling smile. Was he asking her out? Her heart thumped. But she refused to let him think she was some fainthearted, weak-kneed goddessgirl he could win over with one blink of his lovely, long-lashed blue eyes. So she said casually, "Practise? With you? Yeah, I suppose I could do that."

"How about now?"

"Sure," she blurted without thinking. Then she remembered Apollo. "Wait. I almost forgot. I promised to practise with my brother. He's the one who offered to lend you his bow. See, there's this archery competition coming up and—"

"Perfect. I'll learn twice as fast with you *and* Apollo helping me."

"O-okay. But I thought you told Principal Zeus you already know how to shoot."

He shrugged and smiled. "Truth is, I need to brush up on my skills. It's been a while."

Artemis nodded, hoping Apollo wouldn't mind. They practised almost every day, and he enjoyed it when others took an interest in his favourite sport. Maybe if he got to know Orion better, he wouldn't be so hard on him.

"I'll meet you on the field in a few, okay?" Orion looked beyond her. "First I need to meet with my fans."

"Fans?" Artemis turned to see that a half-dozen girls – mortal *and* immortal – had gathered behind her and were waiting to meet him.

He nodded. "There's talk of forming an official Orion Fan Club." He grinned and shrugged again as if to say, *Not my idea, but what can you do?* He took a step away from her and towards the waiting girls, who clustered around him like fireflies to a torch. A collective sigh rose from the group. Sirius plopped down to wait patiently, as if he was used to Orion being the centre of attention and grateful for whatever small scraps of time his master chose to bestow on him.

Artemis glanced around for her brother and spied him still talking to Ares, Poseidon and Dionysus. They were all watching Orion and his budding fan club, shooting disdainful glances his way. Were they jealous? One thing was for sure, they had no plans to join in the adoration. And if she had any sense left at all, she'd make herself quit this crazy crush. But she'd had no experience with matters of the heart until now. She didn't know how to change how she felt about Orion. Or if it was even possible. Or if she even wanted to.

"Ready for practice?" she called to Apollo.

5

Target Practice

"Score!" shouted Apollo, punching a fist in the air as his arrow pierced the centre of the target. "First time I've hit the bullseye from sixty metres. We're going to ace that archery competition this year."

"Yeah ... great one ... bullseye," Artemis mumbled in return. They'd been at it for an hour now, each training their new arrows. Eyes angled towards the school building, she paced back and forth on the archery field behind the Mount Olympus gym. Nearby, her three hounds were napping in the shade of an olive tree.

"Are you looking for something?" asked Apollo, following her gaze.

"Well, yes, actually," she admitted. "I'm watching for Orion. I told him we'd help him practise his shooting."

Apollo frowned. "Why?"

Artemis stopped pacing to stare at him. "He's new here. I thought it would be nice to include him."

"But the competition is coming up. Every practice counts. These new arrows of ours need training if we expect them to shoot true." It was up to each archer to teach his or her own arrows how to best navigate distance and wind currents in order to reach an intended target.

"I know." Stepping up to the shooting line, Artemis aimed her silver arrow at the target. *Zzzing!* Her arrow split Apollo's, and the two of them grinned at each other. "You know we're already the best archers in school," she said matter-of-factly. "And we've practised with every student here at MOA at some point. Why not Orion?"

Apollo wrinkled his nose, looking annoyed again. "I just don't like him."

"Because he's mortal?"

"No!" Apollo exploded, hands on his hips. "Because he's in love with himself!"

"No, he's not," Artemis protested. "Can't you give him a chance?"

Suddenly she heard a dog barking. Sirius ran up to them and began dancing around her heels. Then he bounced off to go and play with her three hounds. She turned to see Orion striding across the field towards them. His walk was cocky and confident, like he hadn't a care in the world. He'd changed into a bright-blue toga that looked great on him. Artemis wondered if, like Aphrodite, he had an outfit for every occasion. If so, perhaps this was his archery outfit.

"If you want to help him try to take the part away from Dionysus, go ahead," said Apollo. "But I'm not going to."

So that's what this was all about! thought Artemis. Her brother and Dionysus were good friends as well as bandmates. "He only wants a chance to practise a little before showing Zeus what he's got," she said reasonably.

"Whatever. I'm out of here," said Apollo. He picked up his bow and arrows in disgust.

"Am I interrupting?"

Artemis whipped round. Orion was standing right behind her. He didn't have a bow or quiver, but he was wearing a pouch clipped to the waist of his toga and was gripping three wooden arrows.

"I was just leaving," said Apollo, shooting him a wide, fake smile. "You two have fun."

"Hey, I brought my own arrows, but if you're not going to need it for a while, can I use your bow?" Orion asked him. The boy had guts, that was for sure. Or maybe he just didn't realise he was pushing too hard. Apollo kept walking.

"Ignore him," said Artemis. "He never lets anyone borrow his bow. Not even me."

"That's okay," said Orion. "I've never understood it, but girls always seem to warm to me more than boys." He smiled, showing gleaming white teeth.

"You may find this hard to believe – I know I do – but not everyone's a fan of O."

"O?" She couldn't help cringing. Ares sometimes talked like this, and she'd always thought him conceited.

"I'm shortening my stage name to O. It's catchier, don't you think?"

"I suppose so," she said uncertainly.

"Ready to get started?" he asked.

Artemis nodded slowly, wondering if she should go after Apollo and try to coax him into coming back. Not only were they twins, they'd been best friends since birth. It felt weird to be arguing with him.

"Listen, I really appreciate you helping me like this, Artie," Orion continued, his eyes big and twinkly as he gazed at her. "You're the best."

Dazzled, she just stood there, a goofy grin growing on her face.

He reached for her bow. "Can I try it?"

She hesitated. Like Apollo, she didn't like loaning her bow to anyone, but if she refused to let Orion borrow it, she was afraid he might not like her. "Of course," she said, pretending it was no big deal. Still, when he grabbed the bow by the string, she was jolted out of her stupor. "Not like that! Hold it by the arrow rest."

"Oh, right," he said, flipping the bow around in his grip. "I knew that." He peered into her quiver, openly admiring her silver arrows. "Can I–?"

"No! You can't use my arrows. I'm training them for the archery competition, and it'd confuse them to be shot by another archer. It's better if you train your own instead."

"I see." Quickly finding the notch in the blunt end, he fitted one of his wooden arrows over the string in the wrong place. Then he drew the bow with his right hand.

Before Artemis could scold him for doing this without getting into the proper position, the arrow's shaft slid sideways off his supporting hand. Falling from his fingers, its sharp tip stuck in the dirt.

Shocked, she stared from the arrow to Orion and back again. It was a good thing Apollo hadn't stayed to watch. He'd be laughing his head off.

"Your bow is different from the kind I'm used to," Orion explained quickly.

"Really?" she asked, intrigued. "I've never seen another kind. What does yours look like?"

"It's hard to explain." His white teeth tugged at his lip as he plucked his misfired arrow from the dirt. "Why don't you just show me how yours is used? Pretend I've never shot one before. I want to relearn everything the way it's done here on Mount Olympus."

"Why?" she asked in surprise as he handed her bow back to her.

"Because Eros is a god. In the play, I want to shoot like he would, not like a mortal."

That made sense. Taking her bow, Artemis stepped up to a line painted on the grass. "Okay. This is the shooting line," she told him. "Stand behind it before raising your bow. Never step over it until you first call out, 'Clear'. If other shooters are nearby, they'll also call out to let you know when they've cleared off the range area."

"That's to make sure no one gets shot accidentally, right?" said Orion.

Artemis nodded. "Of course, our arrows are magic. They wouldn't actually wound anyone if there were an accident. We dip them in the Pool of Magic to make them safe."

"Pool of Magic? Where's that?" asked Orion, listening intently.

"On Earth, in the Forest of the Beasts," she replied. It was thrilling to have his attention completely focused on her. This must be how he felt onstage when the spotlight shone on him.

"That's the setting for the play!" he said, his eyes twinkling again. "Could we go there so I can see it?"

She shook her head. "Mortals aren't allowed in the forest, except during lessons."

His brows rose. "Even though it's on Earth?"

Artemis tried to explain. "It can be a scary place, even for *im*mortals."

"Aw, come on. You're not afraid to go, are you?"

"Of course not," Artemis lied. It was one thing to go to the forest as part of a class exercise with experienced archers by your side. But it would be quite another to go with only a novice for company – and a mortal at that.

"Oh, please. I just want a look," Orion coaxed in his smooth actor's voice. "I won't be able to do a proper job of acting the part if I've never even seen the actual setting. I like to experience what my characters see, hear and feel whenever possible."

He had a point, thought Artemis. And the no-mortals rule was really more of a guideline than an actual rule. Some MOA students were mortal, after all, and they'd been there plenty of times during their lessons. Apollo wouldn't like her going there with Orion, of course. But he wasn't here, so he couldn't tell her what to do.

Besides, they shouldn't encounter any beasts. It was Saturday. If there weren't any classes, Professor Ladon's game would be turned off. "Okay," she said. "Wait here a second."

Dashing to the gym, she grabbed two pairs of winged sandals from the basket just inside the door. When she returned, she gave a pair to Orion. Once they'd slipped their feet into the sandals, the laces magically wrapped round their ankles. Artemis immediately rose to hover a few centimetres off the ground. Orion didn't. "I think mine are duds," he complained.

"They won't work for a mortal," she explained, "unless you're holding on to an immortal."

Orion reached out and linked his fingers with

hers. Her breath stopped and her face went red. He was holding her hand!

"Whoa!" he said, teetering off balance as he rose. He gripped her right hand tightly, continuing to wobble for a minute. But as he began to get the hang of it, he grinned at her. "Wow, I'm pretty good at this."

He has more confidence than anyone I know, thought Artemis. And that was a good thing, right? It was attractive, anyway. People liked confidence in others.

The dogs weren't happy when she told them they had to stay put until she and Orion returned, but she didn't want to have to look out for him *and* them all by herself. Trying to ignore their whines, she grabbed her bow and quiver. "Let's go," she told him. Leaning forward slightly caused the sandals to accelerate. And they were off!

Together they skimmed down Mount Olympus, passing through a ring of clouds as they travelled towards Earth. Orion smiled at her, his teeth shining white as twinkling stars. She smiled back. Had there ever been a more perfect time in her entire life? She couldn't think of one!

"That was mega-mazing!" he told her when they reached the Forest of the Beasts.

"Yeah," she agreed. She was never going to wash her right hand again. A low afternoon fog swirled near the forest and floor and, in the distance, a pool of smooth blue water glistened, surrounded by fantastic plants that wiggled and writhed. Artemis pointed. "That's the Pool of Magic I was telling you about." As they coasted near the ground, a target rose to hover just beside the pool about six metres away from them.

Orion said, "This is the practice area? We shoot at that target?"

Nodding, Artemis guided him even lower. Then she reluctantly let his hand go, and they both touched down. They took off their sandals and pulled out their equipment. "Okay," she said, all business now. "So we're pretending you know nothing about archery?"

At his nod, she patted the wooden parts of the bow, naming each in turn. "Lower limb, arrow rest, upper limb." Then she picked up an arrow and showed him its feathered end. "See the nock?"

He leaned closer, and her heart thumped a little faster. "That's the little groove in the end," he said.

"Mm-hmm." Quickly she showed him how to fit the groove over the bowstring and rest the arrow tip on her non-shooting hand. Standing behind the line painted on the ground, she held up her bow to demonstrate proper shooting technique. Slowly and carefully, she pulled back on the string, sighting along the arrow shaft at the target. "Aim. Then ... release!" When she loosened her fingers, the arrow flew towards the target.

"Bullseye!" shouted Orion. He sent her an admiring glance. "You're good!"

Smiling, she gave him her bow and watched him step up to the line. His form was better this time, but his wooden arrow missed the target by a mile. Although they practised for another hour, she was a little worried about him. Eventually he was able to hit the target, but nowhere near a bullseye. Not good enough to prove himself to Zeus. Though she didn't say so, it looked to her like Dionysus was going to get the part after all. That was only fair.

Both were great actors, but Dionysus's archery skills made him the better choice.

"It's getting late. We'd better go," she said finally.

Orion nodded. "I'll retrieve the arrows." Again he forgot to wait for an all-clear signal. But since they had finished shooting, she didn't scold him.

While he was gone, Artemis located their winged sandals and sat under a tree to put hers on. A soft hissing sound reached her ears. She glanced up at the branches, thinking it was the wind moving through the leaves. But all was still. Then she heard a different sound.

Click! Click! Click!

"What was that?" she asked. When she turned to look Orion's way, her heart began to race. Standing only a couple of metres from him was a beast. One twice his size with crablike claws, eight legs and a shiny black exoskeleton. A giant scorpion! She'd never seen one before, except in her class textscroll. Suddenly, she remembered that Professor Ladon sometimes tested new beasts on weekends. This one must have been sunning itself on a rock beside the pool the whole time they'd been practising, just waiting for them to come close enough to strike.

"Go away!" yelled Orion, waving his hands wildly.

"That won't help," she called. "Stay calm." To her surprise, his face was white and his entire body was quivering. Where was all his confidence now? The scorpion clicked closer to him, curling its tail – its *venomous* tail – high.

Artemis leaped to her feet. Orion was a mortal. He could be killed! Oh, why had she brought him here? For a moment her mind locked up and she couldn't think what to do. He had retrieved their six arrows, but they weren't any good to him against the scorpion without a bow to shoot them.

"*Helllllp!*" Orion ducked low, his hands covering his head, as the scorpion's tail aimed for his neck.

Looked like it was up to her to be brave for the both of them – even though she wasn't feeling very brave at all. Grabbing her bow, Artemis raced towards the unfolding disaster, not sure what she would do when she got there. She reached Orion just as the scorpion struck. Raising her bow, she jammed it over the point of the beast's sharp tail. Surprised, the arachnid forgot Orion for the moment and swung its tail wildly. When the bow shook loose, it flew overhead to land under the tree where she'd left her quiver. *Click! Click! Click!* The scorpion turned on them again, even angrier now.

"We're doomed!" cried Orion. Cowering, he tried to hide behind her. She thought she heard him whimper for his mummy, but she wasn't sure. Something rolled out of the pouch he wore at his waist – his bottle of GodBod! When the scorpion was almost upon them again, Artemis dropped to her knees, grabbed the spray and aimed the nozzle.

Tssst! She spritzed the scorpion, covering it with a beautiful, glittery shimmer. The beast froze, looking stunned. Its image began to flicker, first disappearing from view, then reappearing again, then disappearing.

"What's happening to it?" Orion squeaked.

"Who cares? Run!" Artemis shouted. He took off immediately, still gripping their arrows. A wild sway of the scorpion's tail knocked the spray from her hands as Artemis followed. Her sandals made her faster, and she grabbed the back of Orion's toga on the way, towing him towards the tree.

There, Orion slipped on his magic sandals and she grabbed her bow. Thank goodness it was still in one piece! After the ties laced themselves at his ankles, she took his hand and they sailed back towards MOA, leaving the flickering beast behind.

By the time they arrived, her heart had calmed. "Listen, I really want to thank you for saving me," said Orion as they both tossed their winged sandals into the basket just inside the school's front doors. "You were amazing – as brave as Heracles! Of course, I'm hoping we can keep this whole episode to ourselves. Wouldn't want you to get into trouble for taking me to the forest." He clapped a hand on her shoulder, just like Apollo did to his buddies. His *guy* buddies.

"Right," Artemis agreed, sighing inwardly. Was that really how he saw her – as another guy? A buddy? And why did that bother her so much?

Selecting three arrows from the six he held, Orion slid them into her quiver. "And thanks for bringing me up to speed on archery too. I think I can handle the auditions now."

She stared at him in dismay. Didn't he know how terrible he was? Anyone with half a brain could see he wasn't ready. Maybe the scorpion had scared him out of his wits. Literally. "Are you sure? We could just practise on the MOA field next time, not in the forest."

"I'm sure." Smiling, he slapped her heartily on the back. "Thanks for everything. See ya, Artie." With that, he headed off.

She watched him go, a look of yearning on her face. "My name's Artemis," she said softly. But he was already too far away to hear. Why did she still like him? she wondered. He didn't have the qualities she admired. He wasn't brave or kind, and she had a feeling he sometimes wasn't totally honest either. Still, he *was* cute. Mega-cute. And he was exciting and glamorous too. When she was around him, the whole world seemed a little brighter.

But was that enough? Did it make up for his weaknesses? He *had* been grateful to her for saving his life, at any rate. At least, his thanks had *seemed* genuine and gracious. Any other boy might've been embarrassed to be rescued by a girl. But then, Orion didn't seem to realise she *was* one.

Before she could consider these things more deeply, something cold touched her hand. Dog noses. "Good boys," she said, bending to ruffle the fur on their necks. They'd waited patiently for her return as instructed. "Hey, since you're boys, maybe you can explain why Orion sees me as a pal instead of a girl?"

In reply, Suez barked intelligently and Amby and Nectar studied her intently, their tongues hanging out. Too bad they couldn't talk.

"That's okay. I know you'd help if you could. C'mon," she said. "Let's go and grab some food."

6

Too Much Drama

On Monday during lunch, Artemis was sitting with Aphrodite, Athena and Persephone at their usual table in the school cafeteria. Having already finished their nectaroni, they were enjoying ambrosia sundaes for dessert, when Artemis turned towards Aphrodite. "How do you get a boy to like you?" she asked. As the goddessgirl of love and beauty, Aphrodite was sure to know the secret.

The other girls stared at her in shock.

"I think I'm going to faint," Athena said, carefully setting down her spoon.

"Join the queue," said Persephone. "I mean – Artemis? Interested in boys?"

"Told you it was bound to happen someday," Aphrodite said sweetly.

"But this is Artemis we're talking about," Athena insisted. "The goddessgirl who claims she's going to throw up whenever we start talking about boys or crushes."

"Hello? I'm over here. Listening," said Artemis, waving her hands to get their attention.

"Sorry, this is just so amazing – so unexpected! Are you serious?" asked Persephone.

Artemis nodded, folding her hands on the table.

"Very. There's a boy I like, and I want him to like me back."

"Orion?" guessed Aphrodite.

"How did you know?" Artemis cocked her head, suddenly suspicious. "Hey, you didn't sprinkle me with some sort of love dust to make me like him on purpose, did you?"

"Of course not!" said Aphrodite.

"Then how did you guess who I had a crush on, when even he doesn't know?" asked Artemis, not yet convinced.

"I'm the goddessgirl of love. I notice these things," said Aphrodite.

Artemis sighed. "The problem is, he doesn't seem to know I'm a girl. He slaps me on the back like Apollo and his friends do with one another. He even calls me *Artie*."

"Yikes," said Persephone, giving her a sympathetic look.

When the bell pinged, Artemis got up to throw her rubbish away. The others did too.

"I'll be glad to give you some tips on boys," Aphrodite said, as they all left the cafeteria together. "Here's the first one: when you're around Orion, don't act starstruck. Just relax and be your usual wonderful self."

Artemis gave her a puzzled look. "That won't work. Why would he choose plain old me when he could have any girl? He's got a fan club full of them. And like I said, he thinks I'm a guy."

"Hades liked me better when I stopped acting fake around him," Persephone offered. "I think Aphrodite's right."

Artemis glanced at Athena, silently asking her opinion.

"Don't look at me," said Athena. "I've never had a boyfriend. But I have noticed that boys admire girls who can do things."

"What kinds of things?"

"Things like archery?" Athena suggested pointedly.

Artemis sighed again. The problem was, her friends liked her just the way she was. Well, the way they *thought* she was, anyway. How surprised they'd be to know she wasn't always as confident as they believed! They also seemed to imagine that guys would like the same things about her that *they* did.

"Just keep being yourself. If he doesn't like the real you, he's not worth having," Aphrodite advised.

Artemis nodded and headed for her locker, still

feeling a bit lost and not at all sure she'd learned anything that would help make Orion like her the way she wanted him to. But maybe she was wrong, as the minute Orion saw her in the hall, he rushed up and grabbed her in a bear hug, twirling her around.

"Mega-mazing news!" he said when he set her down. "I got the part! Principal Zeus chose me to play Eros in *The Arrow*!"

Artemis stared at him in astonishment. He'd been awful at target practice. How had he managed to land the lead role when he couldn't even shoot? Beyond him, she saw Dionysus talking to Apollo by their lockers. She felt a little guilty that Dionysus had lost the part, but what could she do?

"I'm going to need your help to perfect my lines," Orion said, snagging her attention again. Looking up into his twinkling eyes, she was dazzled anew by his good looks. This handsome, shimmery guy wanted to hang out with *her* instead of all the other girls he might have chosen? That was nothing short of, well, mega-mazing!

"Okay," she agreed quickly.

Nearly two weeks later, Artemis sat in the amphitheatre after school watching rehearsals for *The Arrow*. Aphrodite and Orion were onstage acting out their parts, with Zeus sitting in the front row giving direction. She hadn't seen Orion shoot yet, but tomorrow was the first dress rehearsal with arrows and costuming, and she was a little worried about what would happen.

"But I don't love you, Eros," said Aphrodite, reciting her lines. "Not really. And you only think you love me. If you hadn't accidentally shot yourself with one of your love-tipped arrows, neither of us would have fallen in love in the first place." She paused, wrinkling her brow like she was trying to remember her next line. The rehearsal was nearly over, and this was the first time she'd faltered.

"I must tell you that I have sworn never to marry," Artemis called out from where she sat, in the centre of the third row, with a script in her hand. Orion had asked her to cue him if he forgot a line. So far he hadn't, but she'd cued the other actors as needed.

"Thanks!" Aphrodite called down to her.

After Aphrodite said her line, Orion continued with his. "That is only because you have been bespelled by a cruel goddess into mistakenly believing you cannot love."

Aphrodite whirled towards him and opened her mouth, preparing to speak her next line.

Only before she could utter a word, Orion went on, "I know you trust me not, for I am a god and you are but a nymph and therefore not immortal."

Artemis sat up straighter, confused. He had changed Aphrodite's line slightly so that it made sense for his character to say it instead of hers! Then he kept going, well past the part he was supposed to recite.

"Those are Aphrodite's lines," Artemis and Principal Zeus corrected him at the same time.

"Yes, I know," Orion told Zeus, flashing his smile. "But don't you think it would be more effective if my character says them instead?"

Zeus shook his massive head of unruly red curls. "Nope."

"But the pathos of it will ring truer if it comes from me, don't you think?" insisted Orion.

"Nope," said Zeus.

"Sounds like Orion is trying to steal Aphrodite's lines," a voice whispered from behind her. Artemis turned to see that Persephone had come to sit behind her.

"He's not stealing them," she protested. "He and Zeus are simply having an artistic difference of opinion." During her script-reading sessions with Orion the week before, he'd explained all about artistic differences of opinion. Apparently, it was something he encountered a lot with temperamental directors. And Zeus wasn't exactly easy to get along with. History was littered with stories of the troubles his mood swings had wrought in the world.

"One other thing, Principal Zeus," Orion said,

drawing her attention. "In the scene where Poseidon is supposed to walk on water, I was thinking it might be more interesting if my character did the water-walk. It would emphasise my godliness. And in the place where Dionysus battles the dreaded scorpion – I think that might work better if I did the fighting."

Behind him, Artemis could see Poseidon and Dionysus glaring daggers at Orion's back. Their faces were so angry that she wouldn't have been surprised to see fire curl out of their mouths, like the dragon Hades had painted on the backdrop.

"For now, let's just carry on according to the script," Zeus told him.

"But–" began Orion.

Zeus held up a big beefy hand. "I'll think about it."

That seemed to pacify Orion for the moment, and

the rehearsal continued. When Zeus dismissed them at the end, Orion went to speak to Aphrodite. Gesturing animatedly with his hands, he said something that made her frown. A minute later she stomped off the stage. Seemingly unaware of his effect on her, he walked towards Dionysus and Poseidon to point out something that seemed to annoy them as well.

Artemis and Persephone jumped up to intercept Aphrodite. "What did Orion say to you?" asked Persephone.

"He keeps trying to give me acting lessons," Aphrodite complained. "He thinks he's the director!"

"I'm sure he's only trying to help," said Artemis. Orion had so much more experience with theatre than everyone else.

Aphrodite frowned. "Well, he's not helping. Would you ask him to stop?"

"Me? Why don't you ask him?"

"I have, but he won't listen. First he won the lead from poor Dionysus. But it looks like that isn't enough for him. He's trying to make his part bigger by stealing all the best lines and scenes from everyone for himself. I'm beginning to think your brother was right about him. Orion's an egomaniac."

"He does seem ambitious," Persephone said as if to soften Aphrodite's remark.

Though his ambition troubled Artemis a little too, she pushed her concern away. "He's used to being a star and—"

Aphrodite cut her off. "Why do you keep defending him?"

"Because . . ." Artemis said lamely.

"Because you like him," said Aphrodite, folding her arms.

Artemis shrugged, a little embarrassed. "Because I think he's mega-tastic."

"Stop saying that word, 'mega'," said Aphrodite. "You're starting to sound just like him. And that's not a compliment."

Artemis glanced at Persephone, hoping for support. After all, no one, including herself, had liked Hades much when Persephone first started seeing him. If anyone would understand what Artemis was going through, it would be her.

But Persephone just shrugged. "Aphrodite's right. All you've talked about for the last week is Orion, Orion, Orion. If anyone says a word against him, you take his side."

"I'm sorry you don't like him," said Artemis, feeling

a little annoyed. "I think he's interesting. Just as you find *Hades* interesting," she couldn't help adding. "Don't you think you could be as wrong about Orion as I – and everyone else – was about Hades?"

"I suppose so," Persephone said uncertainly.

Aphrodite sighed. "Okay, point taken. New topic. So, are we all still on for shopping this weekend? Athena's busy rehearsing with the chorus now, but she said she's up for it tomorrow afternoon."

"Artemis!" Orion snapped his fingers. "Where's my script?"

At the sound of his voice, Artemis jumped. "Coming!" she called to him. Then, in a quieter voice, she told her friends, "Sorry, but I can't make it this weekend. I promised to help Orion with his lines before the play starts next week. You guys have fun without me though."

Aphrodite stalked a few steps away. Then she turned round and glared at Artemis. "First rule of friendship: never, *ever* dump your friends over a guy."

Persephone touched Artemis's arm. "We just don't want you to get hurt. Think about what we said, okay?"

What in the world is she talking about? wondered Artemis. Why would she get hurt? She and Orion were getting along astronomically well, thank you very much. He spent more time with her than anyone.

"Artemis?" Orion called impatiently.

"Got to go," she told her friends, dashing off. *Oomph.* Not looking where she was going, Artemis ran straight into her brother halfway across the room.

"Thought I might find you here," said Apollo.

"Huh?" Then she noticed he was carrying his bow and quiver. She put her fingers to her lips in horror. "Oh no! I forgot archery practice this afternoon, didn't I?"

His expression tightened. "Exactly."

"I'm so sorry. It's just that I got caught up in the play."

Apollo's brows went up. "Since when do you like theatre more than archery?"

She shrugged. "Well ... " Her eyes went to the stage and Orion.

Apollo followed her gaze. His eyes narrowed. "I don't get it. What do you see in that guy?"

"What do you see in that nymph, Daphne?" she shot back.

"Huh? I thought you liked her. She's nice,

and ... " Apollo had the good grace to blush as he realised she'd turned the tables on him. "Touché."

Softening a little, Artemis said, "For one thing, I think Orion's performances are ... magical. He's really good."

"Good at *acting*," Apollo conceded. "Has it ever occurred to you that he might only be *pretending* he likes you to get you to do things for him?"

Artemis took a half step back, as wounded as if he'd shot her with an arrow. He looked sorry for what he'd said, but she didn't give him a chance to apologise or explain. She was too angry now. "Worry about yourself, not me," she told him as she stomped off. "I'll see you at the competition tomorrow morning."

7

Shoot

The next morning Artemis was running late. Frantically she searched her room yet again for the silver arrows her friends had given her for her birthday.

"Opsis! Loxos! Hekaergos!" she called for what seemed like the millionth time. Why didn't her arrows show themselves? Tossing things this way and that, she made one last try at finding them. A knock sounded on her door, and she called out, "Come in!"

Aphrodite flung it open and leaned in. Still in her bright-pink nightie with faux phoenix feathers round the hem, she yawned, looking beautiful even though she'd obviously just got out of bed. "What's all the racket?"

"I can't find my silver arrows," said Artemis.

"You lost something in this mess? How could that happen?" Aphrodite teased. She seemed to have momentarily forgotten yesterday's tiff. Or maybe she was just still half asleep.

"This is important!" insisted Artemis. "I'm supposed to meet Apollo on the Olympic field for the archery competition this morning."

Aphrodite straightened and came inside,

suddenly all business. "When did you see them last?"

Artemis thought for a second, recalling it had been when she'd taken Orion to the Forest of the Beasts. "A few weeks ago," she admitted. As soon as she said it, she realised she hadn't practised archery since then. Every minute of her time outside of class had been devoted to Orion and what he wanted or needed. She'd neglected her friends, her brother *and* her archery. She was even behind in her homework.

"Okay, don't panic. I'll help." Aphrodite dived into the piles of clothing, dog toys, old school projects and athletic equipment scattered across the floor. "Oh, hi, Suez. Hi, Amby, Nectar," Artemis heard her say as she discovered them snoozing under a mountain of laundry. Aphrodite dug deeper, tossing things out of her way: wrinkled chitons and bent scrolls with drawings of dogs that Artemis had made in primary school. Barbells. A broken javelin. A head form with poorly applied make-up and a spiky wig that was so hideous that Aphrodite dropped it in fright.

"Hey! My Year-Four Beauty-ology project. I wondered where that went," said Artemis, picking it up. Giving the wig a fond pat, she then tossed it over her shoulder and continued searching.

Awake now, Artemis's dogs joined in the search, snuffling through the piles. Though they couldn't actually know what they were hunting for, they were always ready to dig.

Eventually Aphrodite emerged from the mess, victorious. "Found them!"

Seeing the shimmering shafts in Aphrodite's

raised hand, Artemis smiled in relief. "Oh, thank godness."

"Why didn't you come when I called, arrows?" she asked as she took them from Aphrodite. They didn't respond, but she didn't have time to wonder why. Quickly she slipped them into her quiver.

She started to dash out the door, but then turned back to look at Aphrodite. "Wish me luck?" she asked. It was the same request Aphrodite had made of her during auditions for the play. Artemis could see from Aphrodite's smile that she remembered.

"Knock 'em dead," she said, giving Artemis the same answer.

Artemis shot her a quick grin, glad that Aphrodite didn't seem mad anymore. "I'm off!" She ran for the door, her dogs at her heels.

"I'll change and be right behind you to watch from the stands," promised Aphrodite.

"Thanks!" Artemis and her hounds flew down the hall, the stairs, and across the school courtyard. Before she knew it, she was on the archery field behind the gymnasium. Zeus, who was going to judge the competition, was already there, along with ten teams of competitors and an audience of onlookers.

"You came," said Apollo, looking relieved when he saw her.

"Of course. I'm your teammate," said Artemis. "I told you I'd be here!"

"I never know with you these days," said Apollo. "And you missed the practice session already. The competition is about to begin."

Artemis winced at his criticism. She knew she'd

let him down recently, but she was determined to make it up to him. As they watched, the first two archers stepped up to the shooting line. Then another team, and another. They were all good, but she and Apollo were better. After the round was nearly over, their turn came. They stepped up to the firing line. It was time to strut their stuff.

"Hey, Artie," someone called.

Artemis looked up. "Orion? What are you doing here?"

"Same as you. Competing." He raised his bow. A quiver was slung over one of his shoulders.

"By yourself?" asked Artemis.

He smiled. "Sure, why not? The rules don't say you have to be a team. I'll just shoot twice as much."

"Mr Big Shot, as usual," Apollo scoffed, but only

loud enough for her to hear. "Is he going to be competition for us?"

Laughter bubbled from Artemis. She put a hand over her mouth, trying to suppress it. "Um, no." She liked Orion, but he was a terrible archer. Why had he even bothered to enter this competition? And why hadn't he *told* her he'd be entering? When Zeus saw how bad he was, he might lose the part. She'd hate for him to be embarrassed like that.

"Artemis? Apollo?" Principal Zeus prompted. "You're up."

Eager to show up Orion and win the competition, Apollo went first. His golden arrow zoomed straight, singing a phrase from one of his band's songs:

> *Nature's music I inspire,*
> *with my gold, harmonious lyre.*

143

Zzzing! "Bullseye!" called Zeus.

"Good work," Artemis murmured as she took his place, preparing to shoot.

"Artemis!" voices called out to her. She glanced to one side and saw that Aphrodite, Persephone and Athena had come to cheer her and Apollo on. Hades, Poseidon and Dionysus were in the stands as well.

Nodding at them, she then turned her attention to the competition and pulled out her first arrow. In the sunlight, she noticed something odd. It seemed a little too glittery. And it was gold, not silver.

"What's up?" asked Apollo, glancing at the arrow. "I thought you were going to use the silver arrows you got for your birthday."

"I was," said Artemis. "I don't know where this one came from, but it's not mine."

"Next!" Zeus boomed, sounding impatient. Artemis had little choice but to use the only arrows she had. She stepped up to the line, took careful aim and released her bowstring.

Zzing! Her arrow flew towards the centre of the target. But a few feet short of its destination, it began to wobble. Then it fell, poking point-first into the ground. It hadn't even managed to reach the target! Artemis just stood there, staring in shock. That had never, ever happened to her before.

"Guess that's why they named you Artie-miss," Orion called out. In the audience, his admirers laughed at his joke, and his smile widened.

"What happened?" Apollo asked her.

"I don't know." Humiliated, Artemis could only stare at the target, replaying her misguided shot in her mind over and over again.

145

"You should have spent more time on the practice field," Apollo chided.

"You know that's not it. It was that arrow!" Artemis protested. "It was trained by a really, really bad archer."

Halfway down the line, Orion stepped up to take his turn. His form was terrible. He had no skill. Yet when he released his arrow, it flew straight and true to pierce the end of Apollo's, in the bullseye.

"Ye gods! He split my arrow right down the middle!" said Apollo. "You're the only archer good enough to do that."

Now that the first round was over, the all-clear signal was given and everyone went to retrieve their arrows from the targets. After picking hers up, Artemis looked at it closely. Something wasn't quite right. She scratched at the shaft with her fingernail.

It wasn't metal – it was wood! The glittery gold was just a coating! And it was exactly the same colour as Orion's shimmer spray.

Understanding struck her like a bolt of Zeus's lightning. That hissing sound she'd heard as she'd sat under the tree that day in the Forest of the Beasts – Orion must have been spraying his wooden arrows with his GodBod! Then, later, he'd put them into her quiver and kept hers for himself.

Orion passed her, carrying the arrows he'd shot and retrieved. A fresh, flowery smell trailed in his wake. *Perfume.* The same perfume Persephone had used on her birthday arrows. So it was true. Orion had *stolen* her silver arrows! The ones she'd spent hours training during target practice with Apollo. No wonder Orion was doing so well! If he'd kept her arrows that day in the forest, he must've used them to try out for the part of Eros too. So that was how he'd beat Dionysus for the lead role in the play!

Artemis's chest felt so tight she could hardly breathe. Orion had cheated to steal the part from Dionysus. He'd taken advantage of her and tricked her. He didn't care about her at all. In fact, he didn't care about anyone but *himself.* As long as he was the star of the show, he was happy. Her friends had been right. But Orion wasn't just an egomaniac, he was a mega-mean egomaniac!

She blinked back tears. Why had she ever liked him? "I'm sorry," she said to Apollo, once she'd got her feelings under control. "It's my fault we're losing."

Apollo shook his head, but there was no time for

discussion. As the second round began, the same thing happened – Apollo hit another bullseye, while Artemis's arrow failed to reach its target. When Orion's turn came, his shot was a bullseye, but slightly off-centre this time. His bad aim was messing up the training she'd given her arrows.

"I hate to admit it, but the guy's pretty good," said Apollo.

"No. He's cheating. With *my* arrows," Artemis insisted. Since Orion had no teammate, he got two shots. As he nocked a second arrow, preparing to shoot again, she elbowed Apollo. "Watch this. If his arrows are mine, they'll obey me, not him." The minute Orion released an arrow, she murmured:

Silver arrow, true and fine.
Hit that boy in his behind!

149

Since the arrow *was* hers, it did her bidding. Making a loop in midair, it reversed direction and zoomed back to nick Orion in the rear.

"Ow! Ow!" Orion exclaimed, holding on to his bottom with both hands and jumping around. "Somebody help! I need medical attention. And a new toga!"

Artemis rolled her eyes. "Oh, don't be so dramatic," she called out.

"Yeah, save it for the stage," yelled Apollo, crossing his arms. "Our arrows are magic. They might sting a little, but everyone knows you're not really hurt. Including you."

Orion did not answer. However, his acting was good enough to stop the competition for a while as others gathered around him in sympathy. In the stands, the other goddessgirls waved Artemis over.

"What just happened?" Persephone asked when she reached them.

"Orion shot himself in the place that hurts him most," Artemis replied.

"His bottom?" asked Athena.

Artemis grinned. "His *ego*."

"That's a pretty big target," said Aphrodite.

They all laughed. Seeing that Orion was alone again, Artemis quickly told her friends, "Thanks for coming out to watch. I'll catch you later." She saw their worried looks as she left them and headed for Orion. They thought she still liked him. Well, they were wrong about that. Now that she finally saw him for the mega-jerk he really was, she was finished with him. Except for one last thing. Running over to him, she snatched her silver arrows from his quiver. "Here," she said, handing him his wooden ones. "I believe these are yours."

"Really? I wonder how our arrows got switched," Orion said in surprise. He was such a brilliant actor that she almost believed his look of innocent confusion. Almost, but not quite.

"Yeah, I wonder," she said, eyeing him so he'd know he hadn't got away with anything. "Now I'm going to have to spend hours undoing the bad training you've given mine. Thanks for nothing." Turning, she stalked off towards her brother. Behind her, Orion limped off the field, still pretending to be injured. Apparently, he was too much of a coward to continue in the competition without her arrows to help him win.

"I don't get it. How did he wind up with your arrows?" Apollo asked when she rejoined him.

"I took him to the Forest of the Beasts," she admitted.

His jaw dropped. "What? Why?"

Artemis shrugged. "It's complicated."

"I'll bet," said Apollo, fuming. Given their poor start, their team lost the competition badly. Artemis could tell that he was furious with her. She wanted to leave him alone until he cooled off, but she made herself do the right thing. Apologise.

"I'm sorry," she told him, sticking by his side as they headed for the stands.

"You should be," he muttered. Waving to Dionysus and his other friends, he broke into a trot, abruptly leaving her for them.

She stood there looking after him, open-mouthed. They'd always supported, defended and encouraged each other, and she'd taken their friendship for granted. But now he was angry with her. She'd never felt so alone, and she didn't know how to patch things up between them. But she did know that fighting over someone like Orion was absolutely stupid.

8

Bailing

When Artemis spotted Orion at his locker on Monday morning, her first instinct was to turn around and march away. She reached down and petted her dogs, thinking. "No," she whispered to Suez. "That would be cowardly. Besides, his locker is only two down from mine. I'm bound to run into him now and then. Better to face him and get it over with." Suez gave her hand a sympathetic lick.

"Artie! Wait till you hear the news!" Orion said when he noticed her drawing near. He was acting as if yesterday had never happened. As if he hadn't stolen her arrows, teased her or cheated. As if he'd done nothing wrong at all. In fact, he was grinning from ear to ear. And he seemed to be cleaning out his locker.

"What news?" She bent to give Sirius a quick pat – after all, he couldn't help who his master was – then she rummaged in her own locker for the scroll she needed.

"Hermes just brought me a message from Earth. The star of the new play in the Dionysia Amphitheatre – the biggest theatre in all of Greece – has got a bad case of catarrh! Coughing, sneezing, the works." He looked delighted that the other actor had a cold.

"And that's good news?" she asked, shutting her locker.

"Yes, because I have been asked to take his place!" Orion had a bag over his shoulder and was stuffing the last of his belongings into it.

With a growing feeling of foreboding, Artemis asked, "Oh? And when does this play start?"

"Right away! Hermes is waiting outside in his chariot to take me to Earth now."

Her jaw dropped. "What? But *The Arrow* starts in just a week."

Orion shrugged. "I'll have to quit." He shut his locker and headed down the hall, with Sirius trotting at his heels.

"Quit? You can't quit!" said Artemis, rushing after

him. "People have bought tickets. Everyone has been rehearsing, making sets. What about the other actors? And your fans?"

"I'm sorry to disappoint my fans, of course, but the offer on Earth is too good to pass up. Besides," he said, rubbing his rear, "MOA is too dangerous for me. What if that arrow had hit me in the face yesterday? It could have ruined my perfect profile. My acting career would've been over like that!" He snapped his fingers.

She didn't bother reminding him that the magic arrows couldn't really hurt him. Instead she followed him, her hounds trailing behind her. "But what are we going to do without you? You're the lead!"

He shrugged again, as if the problems he'd be leaving behind weren't worth his time or attention.

"Don't you get it? This isn't just a school play I've been offered on Earth. It's the big time. My name in torchlights at the Dionysia Amphitheatre."

Artemis pursued him down the polished granite stairway at the front of the school, but she couldn't think of a way to stop him short of tripping him.

At the bottom of the steps, Orion paused and glanced at her thoughtfully. "Hey, I just had an idea! Why don't you come with me? I haven't had much time to study the new script, and you could help me learn my lines." He smiled at her, displaying his dazzling white teeth and his twinkling eyes. He could turn his charm on and off like a nectar fountain, she realised. Well, this time it wouldn't work.

"You've got to be joking. No!" Artemis exclaimed. "You're letting everyone here down. Don't you care?" Part of her was shocked at how she was standing up to him after weeks of letting him run her life. Part of her knew she had to. If he realised how unfair he was being, maybe she could make him change his mind.

"I'm sorry you feel that way," he told her, "but I don't have time to straighten this out right now. Rehearsal starts in an hour, so I've got to head out. You'll explain to everyone for me, won't you?"

Artemis gasped in dismay. "What? You expect *me* to explain to Principal Zeus?" She'd rather face down a beast solo than give the principal such bad news!

Turning away, Orion hopped into Hermes' chariot and told him that he was ready to go.

"No – wait!" She lunged for the chariot. But before she could stop it, it lifted off and sailed away, leaving her to clean up Orion's mess and face everyone's disappointment – again.

"Where's he going?" asked a voice from behind her. It was Aphrodite.

Artemis turned to see her, Persephone, Athena and her brother taking the gleaming granite steps down towards her.

"Orion bailed on our play," she blurted.

"What!" they said in identical tones of disbelief.

"It's true. He got the lead in a big production at the Dionysia Amphitheatre in Greece, so he just took off." She waved towards the chariot in the sky. "Can you believe it?"

"Yes," said Apollo. He glared at her as he folded his arms. Like this was somehow her fault.

Artemis heaved a big sigh. It was obvious her brother hadn't forgiven her for yesterday. As she glanced at the school, her stomach plunged. "Principal Zeus is not going to be happy when he finds out about this."

"Orion didn't bother to tell my dad?" asked Athena, sounding outraged.

Artemis shook her head.

"What a coward," said Persephone, who usually had something nice to say about everyone.

"I guess it's up to me to deliver the news." Artemis began climbing the steps, her heart quaking.

"Are you crazy?" asked Aphrodite, going after her. "You're really going to tell Principal Zeus that his play is ruined?"

Artemis paused. "What's the worst he could do?" she asked, not really wanting to know the answer.

Persephone made a noise in her throat. "*Ahem.*

Have you *seen* his office? Holes everywhere from his lightning bolts?"

"Hey, that's my dad you're talking about," Athena reminded her.

"Sorry, but the guy's got a temper," said Persephone.

Athena shrugged. "Can't argue with that."

Artemis took a deep breath. "But Zeus's bark is worse than his bite, right? He might yell, but he's not going to turn me into a toad or anything."

The others fell silent. Even Apollo. And everyone seemed to avoid looking at her. Hmmm.

Finally Aphrodite spoke up. "Uh-oh. Speaking of Zeus, here he comes."

"Hi, Dad!" Athena called out, as if hoping to put him in a better mood. It didn't work.

"What in thunderation is going on out here?"

Zeus boomed. "Can't a god sleep in for once without someone taking an unauthorised chariot trip?" He was dressed in a long robe with fuzzy slippers that each had big lightning bolts on them. His red hair stuck out in all directions like it was full of electricity. It hardly seemed possible, but he looked even scarier than usual in his PJs as he loomed over their group.

Waving a big, meaty hand towards the chariot that was rapidly disappearing through the clouds towards Earth, he demanded, "Who's responsible for that?"

Dead silence greeted his question. His slipper began tapping. "WELL?" he thundered.

Artemis stepped forward. "Principal Zeus, I have s-some b-bad n-news—"

"SPEAK UP, GIRL!" he roared.

Suddenly Artemis realised that physical prowess in the hunt was only one type of bravery. A different kind of bravery was needed now. Clasping her hands together to keep them from trembling, she looked the principal in the eye. "Orion is gone."

Zeus blinked. "Orion?"

"The foreign exchange student?" Artemis reminded him. "He took a part in another play down on Earth, and he's dropping out of *The Arrow*." She noticed the others were looking at her in awe. Did she sound braver than she felt?

"WHAT?" Zeus's voice was louder than she'd ever heard it. But she refused to cower, even though she was scared. In a way this was like a battle. She just needed to stay calm, keep her wits about her, and face him with as much strength of character as she could muster. "Don't worry. Things are under control." It made her feel braver just to hear her own reasonable, calm tone.

"How do you work that out?" he demanded, folding arms that bulged with muscles.

"Dionysus is Orion's understudy. He can take over Orion's part with no problem," she said, feeling certain this must be true.

Zeus frowned. "Then who'll take Dionysus's part?"

Everyone looked blank.

"Um ... " said Artemis, thinking hard. Drops of perspiration formed on her brow.

"I will," Apollo volunteered.

Artemis looked at him, more grateful than she'd ever been. "Do you know his part?"

Apollo rolled his eyes. "He only had six lines. The part is mostly archery, so how hard can it be?" He clapped a hand on Artemis's shoulder and looked up at Zeus. "My sister and I were practically born with bows and arrows in our hands."

Zeus still looked grumpy, but things were working out so well that he seemed to be calming down. He yawned hugely and scratched his beard. Then he got a familiar, weird look on his face and thumped the side of his head with his fist. "What?" he said. "Yes, well, I'm surprised too, but what can you do? You win some, you lose some."

"He's talking to my mum," Athena whispered to the others. As everyone knew, strange as it was, Athena's mum, Metis, was a fly who lived inside Zeus's head.

Zeus sighed deeply, listening to the voice only he could hear. "Yes, dear. I know you're hardly ever wrong. I was sure that Orion boy was star material, too!" While continuing to carry on a conversation with Athena's unseen mum, he turned on one giant slippered foot and strode back to the academy, the hem of his long robe fluttering in the breeze behind him.

"Thanks, Apollo," said Artemis. "I know you don't even like Drama, so it was really nice of you to volunteer to take over Dionysus's part."

Her brother shrugged. "It was the least I could do. I haven't been entirely fair to you," he admitted. "Part of the reason I've been so grouchy lately has nothing to do with you. I was upset because Daphne sent me a note saying she just wants to be my friend. I should've guessed she didn't want me for a boyfriend. She ducked behind a tree every time I came near her."

Artemis wrapped an arm round his shoulder. "I know how you feel. Really. I'm sorry."

Apollo nodded. "It hurts when someone doesn't like you the same way you like them, doesn't it?"

"Yeah, but that's not all I'm sorry for. I should have listened to you. You were right about Orion, only I couldn't see it at the time."

"He was a jerk, all right," said Aphrodite, overhearing.

Artemis nodded. "A mega-jerk." The others laughed and she smiled, feeling that things were getting back to normal with her friends and brother. It was as if for a time she'd been struck by one of Eros's arrows herself. One that had briefly made her fall in *like* with Orion, just as Eros had fallen in love with Psyche in the play.

But in her case, that love-struck feeling had definitely faded!

9

Wild Beasts

After her last two nerve-racking experiences in the Forest of the Beasts, Artemis dreaded a return there. But she could hardly avoid going when her Beast-ology class was assigned to meet there again the following Friday. She contemplated pulling a sickie, but she didn't want to let her friends down. So, when she could put it off no longer, she stashed her quiver of silver arrows, her bow, a pair of winged sandals and her three dogs in her chariot and called to her four white deer to take them all to the forest.

By the time she arrived, Aphrodite, Athena and Persephone were already waiting, their magic sandals allowing them to hover a few centimetres above the brightly coloured wildflowers growing low on the forest floor. Artemis's hounds hopped out first, greeting the others and sniffing the area excitedly. Reluctantly she slung her quiver and bow over one shoulder and stepped out too. Sitting on a mossy rock, she strapped on her winged sandals. The sooner they got started, the sooner they'd finish, right? She rose to hover next to the others. "Ready," she announced.

Ping! Ping! The faint sound of a bell tinkled, and

a distant voice announced, "Third lesson at Mount Olympus Academy is now in session."

"Just in time," said Persephone. "Let's get going."

Everyone looked at Artemis, waiting. "Somebody else take the lead this time," she said. "I'm not in the mood."

"I will," Athena volunteered, and then they were off.

Artemis brought up the rear, zooming through the forest, her eyes darting here and there. Her heart raced as she watched and listened carefully for telltale signs of lurking beasts.

Clink-clink-clink!

Artemis flinched. "W-what was that?" she called out.

"Godness – you're jumpy today," said Aphrodite, who was just ahead of her. She pointed to a herd of white-bearded goats munching grass nearby. The clinking sound had only been the bells that the nymphs had looped round their necks to keep them from straying.

Artemis tried to calm herself. It wasn't going to help at all if she jumped at the slightest noise. Her favourite bow was at the ready. Her hand flexed on it and her confidence began to build. She could handle whatever came along, she told herself. *Oomph!* Suddenly she bumped into Aphrodite. For some reason, everyone ahead of her had come to a screeching halt.

Looking about, Artemis gulped. Minotaurs had appeared in the middle of their path! Three of them. Each was huge, with horns, clawed hands, hooves, and a gold ring in its snorting nose. They're not *real*, she told herself. They can't hurt anyone. But her traitorous body wouldn't believe her. It insisted on trembling anyway.

"What's going on?" Aphrodite gasped. "Why are there so many?"

Hic! Hic! Hic! All three of the beasts hiccuped at the same time. As if a switch had been flipped, they instantly changed into fire-breathing griffons!

Hic! Hic! Hic! Then they transformed into hippocamps. *Hic! Hic! Hic!* They each turned into a charybdis. And then they were Minotaurs again.

"Something's gone wrong," said Persephone. "They shouldn't be shape-shifting like that."

"Maybe it's some new kind of test Professor Ladon came up with," suggested Athena. In the lead, she was first to nock an arrow and shoot at one of the Minotaurs. Grinning widely, it caught her arrow in its big, scary teeth.

Artemis gasped. "That's never happened before." She and the other goddessgirls began firing, sending off arrow after arrow to no avail. The beasts either caught them or else the arrows sailed right through their bodies to land in the dirt beyond.

"No matter how many times we shoot them, they won't go up in smoke," Persephone murmured. She sounded as scared as Artemis felt.

"There's s-something else w-weird about them," Aphrodite said, her voice an octave higher than usual. Her teeth had begun to chatter, and Artemis didn't think it was because she was cold. "See how they g-glitter? Why are they all gold?"

"Uh-oh." Artemis's eyes widened as understanding dawned. If she was right about what had happened, then this was her fault. And that meant it was up to her to fix things. But how?

The others began to back away from the beasts. They were looking at her as if waiting for her to do something. To rescue them, perhaps? "You know what's going on, don't you?" said Athena. Her face had become as pale as Persephone's natural colour. "Tell us!"

"I brought Orion here a while back," Artemis admitted. "When a scorpion popped out at us unexpectedly, I sprayed it with his GodBod so we could escape."

Hic! Hic! Hic! Just then all three creatures transformed into manticores. One flicked his prickly tail, shooting barbs at them. "Ow!" One of the poisonous barbs sliced into Athena's ankle. She shrieked with pain and fell to the ground. Aphrodite and Persephone dropped down to kneel beside her. Artemis stood in front of them, shooting arrows towards the beasts to keep them at bay.

Aphrodite ripped the barb from Athena's ankle, for once completely ignoring the fact that she was getting dirt on her chiton. "Beasts aren't supposed to be able to wound us. And Athena's really hurt!"

"I'm fine," said Athena, but her voice was weak.

"No, you're not," said Persephone. "You're bleeding. But don't worry, we can sort that out right away." Quickly she began making a poultice from crushed roots and herbs she found nearby.

"Do you think Orion's spray d-damaged the protective mechanism Mr Ladon built into the g-game?" stuttered Aphrodite, eyeing the triplet manticores.

Artemis gritted her teeth, steadily shooting her arrows. But the beasts brushed them off as easily as though they were swatting away flies. "Looks like it."

Persephone placed her poultice on Athena's ankle. "This should draw out the poison, but you're in no shape to fight. We need to get you back to school."

"Any ideas on how to escape those beasts and do that?" asked Aphrodite.

Everyone looked blank. And scared.

"Artemis?" asked Persephone. Aphrodite and Athena looked at her expectantly too.

"I'm thinking." Artemis's mind raced. She had always wondered what she'd do if she was faced with real beasts. These might not be real, but they were certainly dangerous. If she'd ever wanted a true test of her bravery, this was it! Ignoring her fear, she fired again and again, but no matter how well or often she aimed, the beasts continued to advance. As concerned as Artemis was for the goddessgirls' safety, she was also worried for her dogs. They'd been cornered by one of the beasts and were whimpering with their tails between their legs. Now and then she saw her deer peeping through the trees in the distance, too terrified to swoop in and attempt a rescue with the chariot.

"If only there were a way to t-turn off the whole game," Aphrodite lamented.

Thinking about what Aphrodite had said, Artemis reached for another arrow. Realising her quiver was empty, she tossed it away, grabbed Athena's and slung it over her shoulder. "There has to be some sort of on–off switch for these disgusting creatures, and I'm betting it's in the centre of that labyrinth."

"No – you're not considering . . . " said Persephone.

"We're forbidden to enter the labyrinth. We don't know its rules. It's too dangerous."

"And fighting this no-win battle isn't dangerous?" countered Artemis. "Every part of the forest operates separately. No one else – not Apollo or Hades or even Professor Ladon – has any idea we're in trouble here. So weigh up our choices." She shot another arrow towards the creatures, who'd now turned into Calydonian boars.

When it only bounced off one of them, Aphrodite groaned. Reluctantly, she stood and began shooting alongside Artemis. "But even if you get past all of them, how'll you find your way to the labyrinth's centre?"

"I've got to try," said Artemis. Summoning her courage wasn't easy. But they would all run out of arrows soon, so somebody had to do something, and fast. Besides, they wouldn't be in this dangerous situation if it weren't for her. "You keep firing, Aphrodite. That'll keep the beasts busy while I sneak behind them."

Persephone grabbed her arm. "These beasts aren't predictable anymore. We don't know what they're capable of. You could get hurt."

Artemis tried to sound as confident as Orion. "I'll be fine. Hunting is my speciality, remember?" To head off any more argument, she simply left. Stealthily slipping from tree to tree, she skirted the clearing, working her way towards the entrance to the labyrinth. The growls of the beasts, their hiccups, and the swishing sounds of arrows being fired were terrifyingly close, but soon she neared the opening in the prickly holly bushes that formed the labyrinth. Darting from the cover of the forest, she zipped towards it and lunged inside.

She'd made it! Racing down one leg of the continuous path, she rounded a corner and zoomed down another. The path wound back and forth crazily, each portion screened from the others by thick, leafy bushes, which were impossible to see through. "Labyrinth" was just a fancy name for a maze, and she was going to be a-*maze*-d if she ever found her way to this one's centre.

The ground shook behind her. Footsteps. Big ones. Smelled like a manticore. Something hooked the back of her chiton. *Argh!* A giant claw had snagged her, lifting her high. Before her eyes, the manticore began changing, and then she was staring down into the slanty eyes of a humongous, serpentine python. Since it had no arms, it held her aloft with its tail. It grinned, opening wide to display three rows of sharklike teeth. She felt herself moving lower, until her wildly kicking legs dangled just above its lips. She could smell its stinky beast breath and feel its heat too. She was done for. Python dinner.

In the distance, Artemis could hear other beasts roaring and snorting. If she failed in her mission, they would gobble her friends and her dogs. As she neared doom, she noticed something. From this height, she could see the entire layout of the labyrinth. It was a huge square, designed in four symmetrical sections. Carefully, she noted the path to its centre. Then she slid her bow from her shoulder and dropped it into the serpent's waiting mouth. It lodged there, stretching the monster's lips into a ghoulish, bow-shaped, ear-to-ear grin. Immediately, the serpent dropped her to begin using its tail to prise the bow from its jaws. She tumbled head-over-heels through the air, but a few centimetres from the ground she righted herself, and her sandals stopped her fall. Breathlessly, she zoomed away.

Several turns later, Artemis found her way to the centre of the maze, where she discovered a gurgling fountain. Water spewed from the mouths of a three-headed dragon statue, dripping down its scaly bronze body into a pool that encircled it. One of the dragon's mouths was open, breathing bronze fire. That particular head seemed somehow familiar. Come to think of it, it looked surprisingly like Professor Ladon. She yanked off her sandals and waded into the fountain. How was she supposed to turn this thing off?

Boom! Boom! Footsteps. Geryon footsteps this time. The creature was coming after her again.

She hiked up her chiton and shinnied up the long, slippery, swooping neck of the bronze dragon, searching for the on–off switch. There had to be one, but where was it? Stepping higher, she put her foot in the middle head's mouth. *Yeouch!* Dragon teeth, even bronze ones, were sharp! As she moved her foot, she bumped the dragon's tongue. It dropped lower under her weight like a pump handle. Losing her balance, she slid down the statue and splashed into the pool below.

Pop! Pop! Pop! Even underwater, the sounds that reached her ears were distinct. She stood again, dripping wet now. Waiting for claws that never came. What had happened to the Geryon?

"Artemis?" It was Persephone, calling to her from far away.

"Yes!" she called back.

"The beasts are gone!" her friend gleefully informed her.

"Disappeared in puffs of purple smoke," Aphrodite shouted. "Are you okay?"

Artemis breathed a huge sigh of relief. The fountain's tongue must've been the on–off switch for the game! "Yes! I'm coming out," she yelled. Retracing her path through the labyrinth, she was soon reunited with her friends. They hugged one another in relief.

"Whew! This was the hardest A I've ever earned in Beast-ology," said Athena. "Or any other class." Her ankle was fine now. It seemed her wound had instantly disappeared when the monsters went up in smoke.

"Artemis saved the day," said Aphrodite. "Our hero!"

"Hooray for Artemis the brave!" shouted Persephone.

"Thanks," said Artemis. Then, in a move that somehow took more courage than anything she'd just done, she admitted something she'd never thought she'd dare to. "To tell you the truth, I was scared stiff."

Aphrodite threw an arm round her. "Well, of course you were! We *all* were. You would have been crazy not to be."

She was right, thought Artemis. True bravery didn't come from being unafraid, but from taking action in spite of fear. In that instant, she realised that she'd probably always been braver than she'd given herself credit for.

Something nudged Artemis's hand. Suez. He was holding one of her arrows in his teeth. He and the others were okay! "Good boy!" She gave him a pat. "But I don't think we have time to retrieve all the arrows. We'll have to come back later."

"Judging by the angle of the sun, school's over," said Persephone. "We missed our last lesson."

"Oh, no! The play! I've got to go or I'll be late for opening night!" wailed Aphrodite.

"And I'm supposed to sound the first notes with my flute as the curtain opens!" Athena exclaimed.

Putting two fingers between her lips, Artemis sounded a sharp, high whistle. From deep within the forest came her four golden-horned deer, pulling her chariot. They looked a little wary.

"Don't worry," Artemis called to them. "The beasts are gone."

At her reassurance, they zoomed close and touched down. Artemis hopped into the chariot and grabbed the reins. "Come on," she told the others, but Aphrodite, Athena, Persephone and the dogs were already piling in.

Together they whooshed through the forest. Just before they turned upward, towards Mount Olympus, she heard a dog bark. She looked down and saw that her three hounds were resting quietly in the chariot. So who . . .?

Then someone shouted, "Hold up!"

Artemis would have known that voice anywhere. *Orion.* Even though she didn't have a crush on him anymore, her heart betrayed her with a little *thumpety-thump*.

10

Stars

Artemis swooped the chariot lower until it hovered a foot above the forest floor, just centimetres from Orion and Sirius. "What are you doing here?" she demanded. She sensed the tension in her friends. They were in a hurry, and no one seemed ready to forgive him quite yet. And why should they? She wouldn't have thought he'd dare to show his face after taking off the way he had. But as always, Orion seemed oblivious to his effect on others.

"I was trying to find you."

"Why?" asked Artemis in surprise.

He shoved his hands in the pockets of his toga. "My play closed on opening night. They booed us off the stage. Can you imagine?"

An uncharitable spurt of gladness rose in Artemis at the news of his failure. But she did feel kind of bad for him too. "Sorry to hear it," she said.

He shrugged. "Audiences are fickle."

Her golden-horned deer pawed the air restlessly. "Well, we've got to get back to school or we'll be late," Aphrodite said coldly. "Tonight's opening night for *The Arrow*. Remember?"

Orion nodded, looking eager. "Yes, that's why I'm here. Can I get a ride the rest of the way? I want to talk to Principal Zeus before the curtain goes up tonight. To tell him I'm sorry I ran out on the play."

"A little late for that," Athena muttered.

"Better late than never," Persephone quipped.

Persephone was looking on the bright side, but Athena was right too, Artemis thought. Orion should have apologised before he'd ever left MOA. Still, since he was trying to do the right thing now, she was willing to help. "All right. Climb in." Brightening, Orion picked up Sirius as she offered her hand. When he took it, she was delighted not to feel the spark of excitement she'd once felt for him.

Orion squeezed into the chariot, and the other three girls scooted away from him, as if he might have fleas. Artemis grinned. Perhaps he did.

"Hurry!" said Athena. "Let's get this show on the road."

"Chariot, chariot, rise away! Take us up to MOA!" called Artemis. At her command the deer lifted off and they all zoomed skyward. Higher and still higher they went, gliding through the fluffy clouds that ringed the mountainside. Soon the gleaming marble columns of Mount Olympus Academy came into view. And just beyond the school was the amphitheatre where *The Arrow* would be performed. It was a sell-out crowd, with most of the seats already taken. Artemis could feel the excitement in the air.

When they landed next to the stage, Athena dashed to the orchestra pit, while Aphrodite hurried backstage to the dressing rooms. Persephone went with her to help with her hair.

"Good luck!" Artemis called after them. The deer

dashed off, but her hounds were exhausted after their ordeal and stayed to nap in the chariot. Sirius stayed with them, and she decided to sit with them as well, watching as Orion went to speak with Principal Zeus. Zeus's arms were so full of scrolls that he seemed to be juggling them. As he attempted to read his own scribbled notes on one, another would slip from his hands. He'd grab that one, then another would slip. A group of student actors and technicians surrounded him, all asking questions at the same time.

Artemis's eyes widened as Orion pushed through the crowd and tapped Zeus on his muscular shoulder. "Can I have a word, sir?" Though she was feeling pretty brave after her experience in the forest, even she wouldn't have had the nerve to bother the principal just minutes before the show. Now was definitely *not* a good time.

"CAN'T YOU SEE I'M BUSY?" Zeus thundered in reply.

Artemis jumped, and even Orion seemed taken aback at the booming voice. He quickly recovered, though. "But it's important."

Zeus shot him an irritated glance, only then seeming to notice exactly who had tapped him. "YOU? YOU'RE THAT EXCHANGE STUDENT – ORNIE SLAR, RIGHT? WHAT ARE YOU DOING BACK?"

"It's O now," Orion informed him helpfully. "Short for Orion Starr."

"O?" Zeus demanded, raising a quizzical brow. "WELL, WHAT DO YOU WANT-O?"

Cupping his hands round his mouth, Orion stood on tiptoe to whisper something in Zeus's ear that he obviously didn't want anyone else to hear.

Whatever he said made Zeus's bushy red brows ram together in a deep, angry V. "YOU'RE SORRY YOU LEFT US IN THE LURCH-O?" he said, his loud voice filling the theatre. "YOU WANT TO KNOW IF I'LL GIVE YOU BACK THE LEAD ROLE?"

Artemis's jaw dropped. Of all the conniving, double-dealing, underhanded moves! This marked a new low, even for Orion. How *dare* he? She'd never have offered him a ride if she'd known what he planned to do! Orion winced and hunched his shoulders, looking embarrassed that everyone in the theatre now knew what he'd asked. Served him right. They were both risk-takers, she and Orion. But there was a big difference between them. The risk she'd taken in the labyrinth today was to save her friends. Orion took risks only to benefit himself.

"NO CAN DO. THAT PART HAS BEEN FILLED – QUITE WELL-O, I MIGHT ADD – BY DIONYSUS," Zeus informed him.

"Oh," said Orion, looking momentarily at a loss.

Ignoring him, Zeus turned towards the performers and technicians clamouring for his attention. Each seemed to have a problem that required a solution before the play could begin. It must be hard being a principal, King of the Gods *and* a director, thought Artemis. But Zeus was handling it, firing off suggestions and quick-fixes with ease.

Nectar rolled over and put his head in Artemis's lap, and she petted him distractedly. Meanwhile, Orion recovered and began trying to catch Zeus's attention again, jumping up and down and clutching at his sleeve. He just wouldn't give up!

But Zeus continued to ignore him in favour of students who actually did need his help. Artemis saw Hades and a lizard-tailed technician direct his attention upward, pointing at a cluster of seven overhead lights. As Artemis looked at them too, Persephone joined her. "Hades said some of the lights for the grand finale aren't working," she said, staring up.

"I never realised that putting on a play could be so complicated," said Artemis.

When she glanced back at Zeus again, Hades and the technician were speaking earnestly and seriously to him. But Zeus was staring at Orion, who had turned to walk away in dejection, as if he had finally given up hope of regaining the principal's attention.

Zeus shifted the scrolls he was holding in the

crook of one arm and clapped his free hand onto Orion's shoulder. "Ow!" Orion squeaked, as a tiny bolt of electricity from Zeus's meaty fingers zapped through him.

"Hold on a minute," said the principal. He grinned hugely, as if he and Orion were suddenly best friends.

Orion brightened. "Did you change your mind? Can I have the lead back?"

"No. But Hades gave me an idea. I think we can figure out something else – a special part, just for you." Zeus turned and winked at Hades, who only looked confused.

"Mega-tastic!" Orion exclaimed. "I've memorised the entire script and am prepared to play any part."

"Excellent!" Zeus flung his arms round Orion's and Hades' backs.

"Ouch!" they said in unison as he began to lead them both backstage. Seeing his master slip away, Sirius bounded from the chariot to follow.

"I hope you're not afraid of heights," Artemis thought she heard Hades murmur to Orion. That didn't make any sense. Maybe he'd said afraid of *lights*. But that made even less sense.

"Come on," said Artemis, clapping her hands to wake Suez, Amby and Nectar as she hopped from the chariot. "Let's find somewhere to sit before the play starts."

"I wonder which part Zeus will give Orion," Persephone said as they made their way up the aisle of the theatre. "It doesn't seem fair to take a role away from someone else."

"Especially when Orion left everyone in the lurch in the first place," said Artemis. They paused at a fountain, and the dogs lapped from its waters for several minutes. "Zeus wouldn't be that unfair, would he?"

"I wouldn't think so," Persephone said uncertainly.

Once the girls found seats, Artemis settled her hounds beside her. Just as she got them calmed down, the first lovely, clear notes of Athena's flute sounded, signalling that the play was about to begin. After weeks of rehearsal and set building, the efforts of the cast and crew were finally going to be on display. Excitement swelled in her. She could hardly believe the big night had arrived!

The curtain swished open to reveal a backdrop of flower-covered mountainsides with a fire-breathing dragon, a centaur and a beast or two lurking among them. The audience oohed and aahed. Many were seeing it for the first time. Aphrodite walked onto the stage. She was wearing a long, flowing blue chiton that matched her eyes, and there were flowers in her wavy blonde hair. Cue more oohs and aahs.

"Hey." Artemis elbowed Persephone lightly. "Good job with Aphrodite's hair," she whispered. "It's hard to believe she just fought a battle. She looks so beautiful."

"Doesn't she?" said Persephone. Her eyes were shining.

After Aphrodite spoke a few lines, Dionysus appeared onstage. He looked as handsome as always, wearing a white toga and carrying a red-and-gold archery bow. Artemis was relieved to see that Zeus hadn't replaced him with Orion after all.

Aphrodite and Dionysus were so totally

convincing that Artemis soon became lost in the play. She forgot she was watching actors. In her mind, her friends had truly become Psyche and Eros.

"There she is," Eros whispered to himself onstage, spotting Psyche. He crept closer to her as she strolled through the forest, combing her long blonde hair. Stealthily he lifted his bow, aiming a golden arrow of love at the beautiful mortal girl. "May this arrow not wound you, but rather make you fall in love with the ugliest creature on Earth."

A deer ran across the stage then, surprising him the very moment he let his arrow fly. Dropping his bow, Eros accidentally shot himself in the foot with his own arrow. "Yeeouch!" His expression of dismay was so comical and believable that Artemis laughed out loud along with the rest of the audience. Of course this was exactly the way they'd rehearsed it. Eros was supposed to have this accident.

Persephone leaned over and giggled when he shot himself. "Remind you of anyone we know from the archery competition?"

"Hmm?" Artemis was so caught up in the play that the joke didn't even register. She gasped as Eros ran to Psyche's side and dropped to one knee. "I love you," he proclaimed, clasping a hand over his heart. "For ever and ever."

Pandora, in the role of a jealous goddess, swept in from the wings of the stage, her eyes flashing dangerously. "Fool!" she raged at Eros. "To punish you for failing to make Psyche fall in love with the ugliest creature on Earth, I will stop her from falling in love with anyone! In fact, I'll make sure that no one on Earth falls in love ever again – from now until eternity." She paused, then added, "Do you understand me?" Having rehearsed with Orion many times, Artemis knew that this last line wasn't actually in the play. It seemed Pandora couldn't resist asking at least one question.

"Good," replied Psyche, raising her chin and drawing the goddess's cruel gaze. "I'm happy without a boyfriend."

"Yeah! You go, Psyche!" Artemis called out, punching her fist in the air. Persephone and the rest of the audience laughed at her outburst, and she grinned. Seriously, though, before she gave her heart again she was going to make sure she found a really great guy who deserved it.

The story was full of mischief and misunderstandings, and it flew by as fast as the arrows that Dionysus shot from his bow. All too soon it was time for the last scene, in which the trouble was reversed and everyone on Earth was falling in love again. Artemis felt tears burn at her eyes. She'd become so involved in the story that she'd momentarily forgotten that this was just a play. She felt so happy for the characters. If only *she* had been so lucky in love.

As the grand finale came to a close, the orchestra started to play a piece called "Seventh Heaven", written by Apollo's band. Above the stage, a pulley creaked, slowly towing something across the sky backdrop. Suddenly seven bright lights gleamed, suspended high above the actors. No, they weren't lights, but stars. A fake constellation!

"I wonder how they managed to do that," whispered Persephone. "I thought Hades said those seven lights were broken."

"Someone is up there holding them," said Artemis. They squinted into the glare, trying to see who it was. "It's Orion hanging from wires!" she and Persephone exclaimed at the same time. A big mirrored star had been pinned to each of his shoulders and two more were attached to his feet. Those four plus his three-star belt buckle shone brightly, reflecting the stage lights so he looked like a constellation.

Artemis grinned. "Well, Orion always said he wanted to be a star. Looks like Zeus made his wish come true. Times seven."

Persephone giggled, bumping Artemis's shoulder with her own.

Minutes later the play was over and the curtains swept shut. Almost immediately they swung open again, and everyone cheered wildly as the entire cast of *The Arrow* came onstage from the wings. Artemis thought Apollo had done an admirable job as Psyche's father, even if he did have only six lines. She caught his eye. *Well done*, she mouthed at him. Smiling, he nodded, looking pleased.

As the audience cheered and clapped, Suez, Amby and Nectar woke up and joined in by howling their approval. After taking their bows, the actors waved and disappeared backstage.

The velvet curtain whooshed shut again, but the clapping continued. A moment later the curtain reopened to reveal three people: the two lead actors, Aphrodite and Dionysus, with Zeus between them. The three of them linked hands and took another bow. "Ow! Ow!" Aphrodite and Dionysus squeaked in unison as each received a small shock from Zeus's hands.

The audience clapped louder than ever. Artemis was so proud of them that she jumped to her feet. Others followed suit, giving the actors a standing ovation.

11

Friends and Pie

When the curtain calls finally ended, Artemis and Persephone ran down to the stage, followed by three bouncy hounds. The girls hugged Aphrodite and Athena. "Even though I've never seen a play before, I can guarantee that was the best one ever," Artemis declared.

Aphrodite beamed at the praise. "Thanks!"

"C'mon. Let's go and celebrate your opening night!" said Persephone.

"Sounds great. I'm starving," said Aphrodite.

"Me too," said Dionysus, joining them. Apollo and Hades came along moments later, and the three godboys and four goddessgirls decided to go together to get snacks at the Supernatural Market. Aphrodite went to change her clothes backstage before she left, so the girls went with her and the boys walked on ahead.

"Hello?" a lonely voice called out as the four goddessgirls were leaving the deserted theatre at last.

"Who said that?" asked Artemis, pausing to look around.

"It's Orion! He's still up there," said Athena, pointing behind them. Everyone turned to gaze towards the stage. Sure enough, Orion still hung above it on the pulley, his seven stars glittering brightly against the dark backdrop. He looked so handsome there, his stars, eyes and fake golden skin twinkling faintly.

Sirius sat on a bench, in the centre of the front row, watching him as if he thought the play was still in progress.

"Why is he still up there?" asked Aphrodite.

"From the look on his face, I think he's wondering the same thing," said Persephone.

Suddenly Sirius began to howl. "I think there's been some problem with the rigging," said Artemis.

Persephone wrinkled her brow. "Who's going to get him down?"

Several stagehands came out and gathered below Orion, scratching their heads in puzzlement as they stared up at him. Zeus joined them, calling up encouragement to Orion. "Hang up there – I mean hang in there – and we'll have you down in a flash."

"Thanks ... " Orion's lonely reply echoed through the near-empty theatre.

"Do you think we should offer to help?" Athena asked.

Aphrodite cocked her head at Artemis. "It's your call. Do we stay or go?"

Artemis thought about it, then shook her head. "Seems to me Orion's getting the star treatment he deserves." She smiled at her friends. "Anyone else ready for a nectar shake and some ambrosia pie?" Four hands shot up in the air, including her own.

As they turned to continue on to the market, Artemis accidentally bumped into someone. "Sorry," she said in surprise, looking up to see a boy she didn't know. A mortal, since his skin didn't shimmer. He wore a quiver slung over his shoulder.

"Hey, Artemis," he said, bending to stroke a hand over the back of each dog in turn. He glanced at her, his grey eyes steady but curious. "You're Apollo's sister, right? I saw you at the competition. We should practise together sometime."

"Mm-hmm," Artemis said. At her lack of encouragement, the boy just smiled slightly and continued on past them in the other direction.

"He's a friend of Hades. A mortal called Actaeon," Persephone told the group once the boy was out of earshot.

"Cute," Aphrodite pronounced.

"I think he liked you," Athena informed Artemis.

Artemis shrugged. The boy had seemed nice. And he'd actually petted her dogs, something Orion had *never* done. She knew she was brave in some ways, but was she brave enough to try romance again so soon? She glanced back at Actaeon and caught him looking her way too. He waved, and she blushed.

"I see more romance in your future," teased Aphrodite, mimicking the tone of an O-racle-o cookie, a type of fortune cookie served in the MOA cafeteria.

"Ha!" said Artemis, laughing. But maybe she would accept his offer to practise archery together sometime. She'd think about it, anyway. Turning back to her friends, she said, "Speaking of the future, I see some pie in mine. And what about those nectar shakes?"

Giggling, the goddessgirls linked arms and headed out of the theatre in search of snacks fit for the gods.

IN CASE YOU MISSED IT,
READ ON FOR A TASTER OF THE
FIRST BOOK IN THIS SERIES:

Goddess Girls

ATHENA
THE BRAIN

A strange, glittery breeze whooshed into Athena's bedroom window one morning, bringing a rolled-up piece of papyrus with it. She jumped up from her desk and watched in amazement as it swirled above her.

"A message for Athena from Mount Olympus!" the wind howled. "Art thou present?"

"Yes, I'm thou. I'm present. I mean – I'm Athena," she replied in a rush.

Abruptly the breeze stilled, and the scroll dropped right in the middle of her science homework. A thrill swept over her. She'd never received a message from the gods before! No human she knew ever had. The gods and goddesses on Mount Olympus ruled Earth, but only made their powers known for important matters. What could they want? Was she being given an urgent mission to save the world?

She unrolled the scroll as fast as she could and began to read.

DEAR ATHENA,

THIS MAY COME AS A SHOCK TO YOU, BUT I, ZEUS – KING OF THE GODS AND RULER OF THE HEAVENS – AM YOUR FATHER. AND THAT, OF COURSE, MAKES YOU A GODDESS.

"Huh?" Athena's knees wobbled so hard that she plopped back into her chair. She read on:

YOU MUST BE, WHAT ... NINE YEARS

OLD NOW?

"Try twelve," she mumbled under her breath. And for most of those years, she had yearned to know who her parents were. She'd spun endless stories in her head, imagining how they looked and what they were like.

At last a piece of the puzzle had dropped into her lap. Or onto her desk, anyway. Her eyes raced across the rest of the letter as she continued:

AT ANY RATE, YOU'RE PLENTY OLD

ENOUGH NOW TO CONTINUE YOUR

SCHOOLING AT MOUNT OLYMPUS

ACADEMY, WHERE I – YOUR DEAR OL'

DAD – AM THE PRINCIPAL. I HEREBY

COMMAND YOU TO PREPARE AT

ONCE FOR THE JOURNEY TO MOUNT

OLYMPUS. HERMES DELIVERY

SERVICE WILL PICK YOU UP

TOMORROW MORNING.

YOURS IN THUNDER,

ZEUS

Was this for real? She could hardly believe it! Beneath his signature was the worst drawing she'd ever seen. It looked sort of like a caterpillar, but Athena had a feeling it was supposed to be a muscled arm. She grinned. One thing was for sure, Zeus was no artist.

A blazing gold Z shaped like a thunderbolt – Zeus's official seal – was embossed alongside the drawing. She traced her finger over it.

"Ow!" A burst of electricity buzzed her fingertip, and she dropped the scroll. As the sizzle zinged through her, the scroll shut with a snap and rolled across the carpet. No question about it, this letter was from the King of Mount Olympus!

Feeling dazed – and *not* from the electricity – she gulped. She was his *daughter*. A goddess!

Athena jumped to her feet, unsure if she should be happy or upset, but feeling a little of both. Rushing over to the mirror, she gazed at her reflection. Her determined grey eyes stared back at her, looking no different from before she'd read the letter. And her long, wavy brown hair was the same too. With a poke of one finger, she squished the end of her too-long nose up, then frowned at the piggy nose she'd made.

She wasn't sure what she'd expected to see in the

glass. To suddenly look beautiful, wise and powerful? In other words – more like a goddess?

She turned as she heard her best friend Pallas come into their bedroom.

Crunch! Crunch!

Pallas eyed her, munching an apple. "What's that?" she asked, gesturing towards the letter on the floor.

"Umm." Athena quickly scooped it up and tucked it behind her back. Looking suspicious, Pallas came closer, trying to see what it was. "Come on. Give. I've known you for ever. Why are you suddenly keeping secrets?"

Athena thumped one end of the scroll gently against her back. On one hand, she wanted to twirl around and shout the news that she was a goddess! At the same time she wanted to hide the letter in the back of her wardrobe and pretend it hadn't come.

Zeus's summons was going to change *everything*.

"It's a letter," she finally admitted. "From my dad. Turns out he's ... Zeus."

Pallas stopped in mid-munch, her mouth full of apple. "Wha? Zeu?" Quickly she finished chewing and swallowed. "Your dad is the King of the Gods?"

Athena nodded, holding out the papyrus scroll.

Pallas pounced on it. By the time she finished reading, her eyes were huge. "You're a *goddess*?" Her voice rose to a squeak on the last word.

"I don't want this to change things," Athena said quickly. "We'll still be best friends, right?"

Pallas examined the scroll closely, seeming not to hear. "Who brought it?"

"The wind."

"It's got the official seal and everything. It's the real thing, then – an invitation to Mount Olympus." Pallas stared at Athena in wonderment. "My best friend is a goddess!"

ABOUT THE AUTHORS

JOAN HOLUB says that of the four Goddess Girls, she's probably most like Athena because she loves to think up new ideas for books. But she's very glad that her dad was never the headmaster at her school!

SUZANNE WILLIAMS asked her husband what she was the goddess of, and he said "of asking silly questions"! (Suzanne says they're mostly about why her computer is misbehaving.) That makes her kind of like Pandora, except that Pandora never had to deal with computers. Like Persephone, she also loves flowers, but she doesn't have Persephone's green fingers.